Feel at Home

Elle Brownlee

DREAMSPINNER PRESS

Published by
DREAMSPINNER PRESS

8219 Woodville Hwy #1245
Woodville, FL 32362 USA
www.dreamspinnerpress.com

This is a work of fiction. Names, characters, places, and incidents either are the product of author imagination or are used fictitiously, and any resemblance to actual persons, living or dead, business establishments, events, or locales is entirely coincidental.

Feel at Home
© 2024 Elle Brownlee

Cover Art
© 2024 L.C. Chase
http://www.lcchase.com
Cover content is for illustrative purposes only and any person depicted on the cover is a model.

Trade Paperback ISBN: 978-1-64108-778-0
Digital ISBN: 978-1-64108-777-3
Trade Paperback published September 2024
v. 1.0

Readers Love ELLE BROWNLEE

Say Yes to a Mess

"Fans of the fake engagement trope will love this sweet love story…. If you enjoy reality TV, fake marriage, and a sweetheart main character, this is a great book to pick up."

—Rainbow Book Reviews

Two for Trust

"Read. This. Book. And then re-read this book…. Apparently, this is the MM Romance novel I've been looking for."

—The Oddness of Moving Things

Force Play

"If you are a fan of baseball you will LOVE, LOVE, LOVE this!"

—Open Skye Book Reviews

"This was a good story—I enjoyed the characters and loved cheering for the underdogs."

—Inked Rainbow Reviews

Emergency Contact

"The two together make a great couple. In fact, they are the perfect formu-la for a nice story that will have you rooting for their HEA all the way to the end."

—Hearts on Fire Reviews

"I did not want to leave these two. Even through their sometimes prickly, sometimes quiet stubbornness I felt an inexorable warmth and rightness radiating from them."

—It's About the Book

By ELLE BROWNLEE

Cardinal Christmas
Cliche Christmas
Drawn
Emergency Contact
Feel at Home
Force Play

DREAMSPUN DESIRES
Off-Map Hearts
Two for Trust
Say Yes to a Mess
COAST GUARD RESCUE
Staggered Cove Station

With Tere Michaels and Elizah J. Davis
One Holiday Ever After
One Night Ever After

Published by DREAMSPINNER PRESS
www.dreamspinnerpress.com

Chapter One

"YOU SAID you needed three things." Tom stacked their dishes and rose from the breakfast nook table to carry them across the huge, sunlit kitchen and drop them in the sink. "Feeding you lunch makes one." He leaned a hip on the counter and crossed his arms expectantly.

Philip drummed his fingers and nodded. The other two things were straightforward, necessary. Asking was hard. "Help me sell the house and let me store my crap in your barn for a while."

"Shit, man. What?" Tom shook his head in disbelief, closed his eyes, and then held up his palms. "Okay, okay. I'm not reacting, and don't get into it yet. This requires coffee."

Philip listened to the familiar rhythm of Tom busy with an ancient percolator. If he wasn't mistaken, the coffee maker dated back to their dorm days. He drew his hands up and rested a cheek on knitted fingers and watched the pretty and mundane day out the window. The loping dark shape of ancient mountains covered in trees, the nestle of Tom's fields and pollinator lawns still dormant in this early spring, clouds and their shadows lazily floating across it all.

His gaze flicked to the barn he'd asked about, huge and broad, red-blond stone and timbers that could cheerfully hold a ton of burden. He allowed himself the whimsy that it reminded him of its owner.

It would be more than big enough for the few things he was determined to keep.

Tom set a steaming mug in front of him—light with "too much" milk and sure to be sweet—and settled into his chair. He leaned back and rested an enormous college logo mug on his middle, had a deep drink, arched a bristly red brow, and waved Philip to go on.

When they'd met, Tom had been a strapping farm boy who'd only gotten bigger playing football. Since then he'd softened into a burly dadbod. It suited.

"Right. So…." Philip also had a drink, perfectly sweetened, mostly to stall. This shouldn't be difficult. Tom was his best friend, knew everything about him, sitting there doubtless already cranking through ideas and options and rescue plans. He had another drink. Stupid talking, stupid feelings. "It's simple math. I can't afford the house and that means sell it, and sell it means I have to do something with my stuff."

"I can find some hours for you. Float you a loan? Crowdfund? You could rent it for a while, see what comes together after that." Tom made a short, annoyed sound. "Me telling you what you've already thought about doesn't do much good here."

"No, it's fine." Philip sighed. "But then after any of that, what? Borrow more and beg again and who's going to rent that house, anyway?"

"Open a quaint bed and breakfast?"

"My house is small. Slinging yogurt at strangers and sharing the bathroom on the off-chance I'd get enough business—any business—isn't my kind of delusion. No. The wound is too big. I can't bandage it any longer."

Tom wiped coffee from where his mustache and beard met and hunkered forward on his forearms rested on the table. "You didn't have to pay for the burial."

"No, I sure didn't." Philip shrugged. "But then again, didn't I?" He couldn't explain why he'd felt responsible for that, for a mother he'd written off years ago. Some mix of closure and spite and the last of a foolish, lingering sentiment it mattered.

"At least Kelly got you out of the bills and debts. At least you let her." Tom's gaze lightened at the mention of his wife.

"Eh, she's a better lawyer than you."

"A lot of people are." Tom smiled easily, because they both knew he was far from mediocre. "That… *mother* of yours," he said tightly, like a curse.

Philip winced.

"Hey, I'm sorry."

"No, it's cool. We both know it's the truth." She'd never mothered him, never wanted him so far as he could tell. Tom had seen a lot of that—Philip had gone to a school on scholarships and grit far away from home, as much to get far away from her as anything.

"I understand you never want to talk about all that, about her and dumb feelings and everything, but if it ever changes you know I'm around. Okay?"

"Okay. Thanks." Philip appreciated Tom's concern and offer. It would never change.

They'd made unlikely friends the moment they'd clapped eyes on each other when Tom had barged into the tiny dorm room they'd shared their freshman year of college. They'd remained roommates from then on, neither having the means for apartments, even if Tom went to the parties and Philip hid from Tom to avoid them.

Philip had been a string bean back then, lean but strong from years of odd jobs and kitchen work and day labor, dark hair longer than he wore it these days. He preferred walking for miles in the dead quiet of night, always taking his pictures, bookish and reserved. He'd braced for rejection or worse when he'd told a virtual stranger—a handsome and gregarious country-and-sports guy—that he was gay. Tom had taken it in, nodded, and made him do a high-five promise pact that he'd be open to dating a teammate if Tom found "a good one."

Tom had come to college to play football, tore his body up bad, and then actually had to study. Philip guided Tom through that rough transition and turned him into a decent student. Philip had wanted a degree for the promise of stability and a way out, and then had trouble staying put for four years. Tom had kept him anchored just long enough to graduate.

"Are you absolutely decided on selling?"

"Unfortunately." Philip finished his coffee and went to get more.

He'd lived through his fill of skipping out on rent, the inescapable dread and shame at the heavy knock of the sheriff there to evict you, dragging what you own around in a plastic bag until even that becomes too much so you decide owning anything is for chumps.

Never again. Even if it meant the loss of the house, the home he'd at last started to carve out for himself. He nabbed a notepad and pen and brought the pot back to the table and slid all of it closer to Tom's side.

Tom grunted thanks and picked up the pen to doodle.

"It wasn't only the burial, you know. If it was only that, I'd have figured it out." Philip licked his lips and forcibly disengaged from the obsessive what-ifs that wanted in. He might not do regrets, but his brain was always eager to supply looping, endless scenarios of what could have been done differently. Survival had instilled that in him, and it saving him more than once made it a tough habit to break. "It was everything at once. Including relocating that family of raccoons who'd happily chewed through three roofing joists."

"I hear you. Moving from the city, giving up some gigs, and you had sizable savings from living so cheap for so long, but it only goes so far when thrown at making a moldering house livable again." Tom drew tiny interconnected waves and finished one with a flourish to then frown at Philip. "You can't hold on long enough for your book?"

Philip's gut churned but he smiled lightly. "The market's not good right now, so the book's not good right now. As it stands, no one wants a doorstop full of glossy pictures of grim situations and my pithy stories to go with them."

"You're absolutely sure? We can afford to help bridge that gap."

"Not enough, and I don't want to start owing on top of everything else, even if it's you guys." Especially them. Banks were cold numbers and all business, and Philip could handle that. He wouldn't risk adding friction and complications to the only good and stable relationship he had.

Tom kept staring at him, clearly unconvinced.

"That's how it goes sometimes. Writing and photographs are fickle," he said with lack of care but enough certainty to dismiss the topic.

Writing and photographs had gotten him the down payment and savings to drain. But it couldn't do everything. He pushed all he'd failed to do with the book down, hidden away. He blanked out the memory of returning the advance and the messages from Eric—his editor at the prestige publisher who'd wanted the book—he never answered. He pretended it didn't matter, that his mother reaching out just to tell him she was dying hadn't sent him into something of a tailspin and that he hated his own weakness to have been affected enough to blow the book deal and all the opportunity it represented.

The loss was no big deal, same as the house. He had to convince himself of that, at least. So, he deflected.

"Eh, this proves I was right and settling down isn't for me. It's time I get back to having a real life."

Tom raised both arms and gestured around them. "This is a real life."

"For you it is. And it's been proven not for me. We talked about that when I bought the place, remember? The house was the fever dream, not living out of a tiny duffel on hard candy, pistachios, and camera equipment."

Tom grumbled and opened the tin of cookies that was always on the table.

After they'd graduated, Tom had wrangled good scholarships to Yale and became a bigshot lawyer. Philip had rambled, needed to move, and his vague but solid liberal arts degree, ability to learn on the fly, and bold restlessness let him take gigs writing copy and taking pictures for any newswire service he could scrape a living from in all the places he wanted to go. He didn't know anything else but to grab hold of what worked in the moment and ride it until it was too thin to hold anymore, and then move on to the next thing.

He'd never figured the next thing would eventually be that house in Tom's hometown. Philip was familiar with it thanks to Tom's stubborn insistence he tag along during breaks and holidays. Tom's parents had taken him in as readily, and so he supposed that made this the closest thing he had to a hometown.

During one of those breaks they'd discovered it while on a hike, and he'd talked Tom into breaking in to explore on the pretense of needing a subject for his current photography independent study.

They'd shouldered into a water-warped side door and Philip had felt suddenly, oddly, at home. He couldn't explain the attachment or the want to own it, fix it up, live in the creaky-floored rooms and overlook the river winding in the below valley. Sometimes things had no explanation other than they simply were, and Philip wanting that house ranked among them.

But Philip had ignored the strange knowing. There wasn't space in his life for such an impulse—such an impulse had always turned out to be dangerous and stupid and punished him in the end—and he couldn't give up chasing down hot wars and cold reality for an abandoned house in the middle of nowhere. He'd kept rambling, and Tom made a go of it in Boston.

Eventually Philip had a crash pad in New York City, Tom met Kelly through work, and then a few years ago Tom had moved back after his parents decided to downsize. He and Kelly sick of racking up billable hours chasing partner and wanting a rambling yard for the kids they wanted to have. The first of those was due in a few months.

A year ago Tom had texted the listing to the house—*his* house—and offered the upstairs of their quaint downtown law office building until he'd rehabbed the house enough to move in.

Philip had been between wars, funding, natural disasters, an editor who gave a shit, adrenaline, desire. Whatever it was that kept him going. More than anything he'd been tired. Learning he could afford the house had been the worst part.

Giving in to the whisper of possibility of having somewhere to slow down, quiet the noise, and feel safe had been the most dangerous.

"What's knocking around in that broody brain of yours?"

"The usual." Philip grabbed a cookie.

"Hmmph, great." Tom tapped the pen on the pad. "I ran some numbers. Do a For Sale By Owner. Kelly and I will help with the paperwork and closing and all, and then you're not out commission money. Plus, she knows everyone around here and rich city people who want a country house."

Philip laughed. "Like you guys?"

"We have a house, and we chose to leave for good, not for long weekends. You need extra wealthy rich city people who won't bat an eye and pay cash for the full, not little homesteaders and small-town lawyers like us." Tom sighed. "Anyway. She'll bust some buyer's balls to get top price, which have gone up even since you bought, and you know, you bought a shell and now it's habitable. That'll be enough to get you square at least."

"Should I repaint or anything? I've never sold, well, anything before."

"Nah. You have good taste, I mean what I think is good taste. And people don't turn down houses because of accent walls. They want it or they don't—you bought it before it had plumbing and electricity working."

"Fair point."

"And after it sells? Then what?"

"Stay until Kelly has my niece so I can at least meet her and then…." Philip gestured expansively. "Maybe I really am never meant to grow moss."

"And maybe there's another solution. It's possible." Tom frowned. "We asked not to be told the sex of the baby, so we don't know yet."

"Yeah, yeah." Philip rolled his eyes. Everyone knew Tom was getting a girl and that Tom would absolutely adore and spoil her. "As for any other solution, I've lost enough sleep and writing painstaking lists to admit there isn't a last-ditch save here, and I've accepted that."

"Well, it sucks. You just got here, and it's been great to finally have you around for more than a long weekend and it sucks." Tom glanced out the window and worked his jaw and then looked intently at Philip. "I'll miss you. A lot. And don't tell me not to say that."

Philip rolled his lips in and nodded. He'd miss this a lot too.

They sat kinda glumly until Westminster chimes sounded from the living room.

"If I hustle, I can get pictures of the house and yard in the golden hour. People will fall over themselves to pay premium just from that," Philip tried to joke.

Tom indulged his effort with a smile and walked him through the house. On the front porch they were swamped by three enormous and happy farm dogs who accompanied them to his car.

"Do you want help with the listing? I think Kelly has done one or two."

Philip shook his head. "I've managed to wire stories halfway around the world using a flip-phone from the jungle. I think I can manage posting a house for sale."

"Reach out if you somehow can't. And text me when the listing is live—I wanna see these golden hour shots of yours. Text me if you're not sure about anything. Just." Tom clapped a broad hand on Philip's shoulder. "Text me, okay?"

"I promise." He could tell Tom was weighing the possibility of grabbing him in for a rarely allowed bear hug, but even with the crap news and crappier mood it created, he didn't want one. But he did whap his hand over Tom's before dropping into the driver's seat. "Thanks."

"Of course—always! We'll figure this out." Tom closed the car door, gathered the dogs, and walked backward toward the house. "And stay open to alternatives. You never know." He tripped on a boulder in the landscaping but recovered nicely.

"I'll agree if only so you don't kill yourself before your daughter arrives. Yeesh." Philip shooed Tom and waited until he'd disappeared into the house, the dogs and glimpse of their tabby cat streaking in after.

The drive to his—almost not his—house was twenty minutes on a clear and easy day, following the river and then cutting up into the forest to a perch on a carved-out foothill. He parked and then paced a very slow circle to look around and take it all in. Then, instead of indulging in any moping or regret, he grabbed his gear and got busy.

He treated it like any other assignment, removing self from the environment, and with a constant eye on vantage point and scale and frame to get exterior and landscape shots. Philip captured the front of the house backlit by a magnificent sunset, and as he stared at it on the camera display, he couldn't hold in a brief, bitter sigh.

The house wasn't huge or of any historical importance. Four bedrooms in a two-story fieldstone box, one side taller than the other, distinguished by a tall crooked chimney, white trim and a small A-frame up façade that hugged the dark red arched front door with its moon cutout, and small porch. Mature trees close on all sides.

It sat on twenty-five acres. A huge parcel that felt small, and that big because the land buckled with veins of granite was considered useless, but was left with just enough space for the house and a diagonally shaped yard surrounding it. The rest was a wild tangle of forest, and about fifty feet from the back patio, it dropped off in tumbling layers down to the river.

Nothing special and entirely magical. He'd never been able to fight its pull, that just-something-about-it. He hadn't stressed himself trying to explain it either. In truth he wasn't sure he wanted the answer.

Philip trudged inside and got pictures of the patio, the windows overlooking the patio, and then the rest of the rooms. He took detail photos of the potbellied stove in the front parlor, the fireplace, intricate woodwork on the stairs and molding, slide-over shutters in the upstairs bedrooms with their bird-shaped stays.

Before he'd known his finances—and then whole life—would be upended, he'd sunk a pretty penny into modernizing the heat, air, and plumbing. He supposed that'd be worth it in the asking price he could demand.

The one thing the house lacked was decent internet and cell reception, but if he sat in the tiny northeastern bedroom at his desk shoved under the front window, he got bars and the best signal strength from the satellite. He sorted the photos—good ones but not good for a listing, bad ones outright—and narrowed it to twenty. While he'd been busy with the photoshoot, Kelly had sent him links for various ways to list the house, sale by owner, and said to put her name and number down as a contact.

He for sure would.

Philip might be able to take in stride this had to happen, but that didn't mean he wanted to take calls from strangers eager to move into his house, to haggle over the price, to know he had to sell it. He couldn't imagine anyone would pay the listing price he aggressively set—it was well over what he'd paid—but that much would be nice to get. He might as well try. It'd go a long way to helping him dig clear and have something to live on as he started over. Again.

He finished the last of four listing sites he'd decided to bother with, pushed from the desk, and kept moving. Moving was purpose and purpose was good. The air outside had chilled and wafted into the house. Instead of closing windows he made coffee, got into a thick hoodie, and carried it to the big bank of windows to watch the last strong light of the sun settle into dusk over the backyard.

Philip palmed his phone from a back pocket and thumbed it awake as it vibrated.

Holy shit.

You already have an interested buyer!?!

They're driving over like right now.

His pulse surged as he read Kelly's texts and he pivoted, stashed his mug in the kitchen sink, and then he took two steps and stopped because he wasn't sure what to do next.

Really? Should I leave or?

He left it there and then went to turn on the front porch light.

I said I'd meet them there if you don't mind. They're cool with you being home but just go hide in the bushes if that's easier.

"Talk about eager," he breathed. Where had they even come from?

Philip slung a heavier coat over his shoulder, ran around turning on all the lights, retrieved his coffee, and fired off a final text to Kelly as he exited the back door. He warned her he probably wouldn't have a signal once he was out of the house and that yes, he was definitely going to go hide in the bushes.

He headed straight for a huge, flattened rock with another huge rock angled beside it breaking from the tree line. The first day he and Tom discovered the house, they'd napped on them in the sun and he'd thought of them as a safe little hideaway ever since. There he'd be out of sight from the house unless someone really scoured the woods.

The coat made a cozy and soft cushion and he stretched out, back to the angled rock, legs crossed at the ankles. He sipped the tea and tried to relax but was too aware of everything. How sudden Kelly's texts had been and then how long it seemed to be taking them to arrive. Noises in the underbrush and the light breeze in the treetops. The weird, ghostly negative effect of the house shrouded in the coming evening with all the lights blazing inside.

Gravel crunched in a rhythm that wasn't syncopated, and then doors slammed and Philip's heart tripped again.

Kelly's voice, and then voices he didn't—wouldn't—recognize.

Shadows and movement progressed through the house. A large figure appeared in the back window, exactly where he'd stood not even a half hour ago. The door slowly opened and the figure almost tiptoed onto the patio. Philip couldn't make out the man's face but the guy planted his hands on his hips, tipped his head back, bodily relaxed, and exhaled loudly enough for him to hear.

He knew the feeling—how perfect that spot was, calming and invigorating simultaneously. It was oddly reassuring the guy "got it," and oddly disconcerting too.

A woman joined the man, and he strained to hear their murmured conversation but couldn't catch anything meaningful. She tugged his arm and returned inside. The guy stayed a moment longer and then followed her into the house.

It seemed like hours before an engine coughed in the dark quiet and a car drove away.

"Philip? Come on out, it's safe," Kelly called from the patio.

He checked his phone. It hadn't even been forty-five minutes.

Kelly waited for him and paced the width of the house where it all opened in a single run. She made a slow figure eight, from the far wall and fireplace, cutting through the clusters of chairs and tables that comprised the living room, to the seating bar boxing in the kitchen at the front of the house, and back to the fireplace. All under a graceful barrel ceiling he'd painted a warm white that carried long and narrow banks of warped-glass pale green and yellow paned windows on its tall shoulders.

He made her peppermint tea and sat on the arm of one of the wide leather chairs. "Well?"

"Oh! Sorry. I'm expecting their text. They wanted to discuss a few things on their own."

Philip plunked his mug on the huge desk he used as a dining table, grabbed her phone and ran upstairs with it, and held it against the bedroom window. After it buzzed several times, he ran back downstairs.

"I knew that but I always forget. Also—pregnancy brain." Kelly rolled her dark eyes and blew a strand of long, inky black hair from her forehead. Everything that Tom was she wasn't, but they made a perfectly suited pair. As she scrolled, her eyes widened. "They want it. Full asking price. Ready with the down payment and don't expect financing to be a problem."

"Wow. That was… fast." Philip rubbed his chest, stopped and let out a slow breath, and schooled relief and dismay into purpose. "Right, okay. Just like that?"

"Just like that, barring a bad inspection and no major repairs. I said you'd agree to credits if they found anything worrisome." She tilted her head. "They won't, will they?"

"No. At least I don't think so, given how much work I've put in."

Kelly made a sympathetic sound. "Tom told me all about it of course and, well, it's all just a stinky pile of burnt sugar with lint stuck to it. I'm so sorry."

Her description of the situation pulled a chuckle from him. Tom had once said she was the only lawyer he knew who refused to curse.

"Thanks."

"This is so sudden, even with you braced for having to sell pronto. If you need to stay with us, of course you're welcome. Or you can crash above the office again—we're kind of an explosion of baby at the moment." Her eyes widened and she gripped her belly to moan, "Oh, baby explosion—you'll miss her first steps!"

"Above the office would be great, as it seems I'll have to." Philip pointed at her mug. "More?" She was easy to distract with promises of food these days, and he didn't want to get into missing first steps or her and Tom or letting her get weepy over anything.

"Hmm… do you have anything peachy and cinnamony and creamy? And maybe with chocolate."

"No."

Kelly pulled a face and Philip lifted his hands. Tom had advised early that indulging and coming up with an approximation seemed to work better with preggers-Kelly than outright denial.

"Okay, I'll see what I can whip up."

"Super!" she said cheerily, her dark cloud already cleared. She made another figure eight and stopped at the bar, smiled, and patted her belly. "I feel best when I'm distracted and busy these days, and this gives me something to do, so don't go worrying that it's an imposition. Also Tom never lets me forget we're forever in your debt for not letting him fail out of college. Even without that, it's the least I can do if for no other reason than you did spend a week painting and repainting, and then repainting, the nursery for me."

"Fair." Philip scrounged for what might work and invented hot cocoa with peach preserves melted in it, a ton of creamer added for good measure, and the top coated with cinnamon. "Something like this?" He set the steaming mug on the dividing bar for Kelly to take. "I dunno, it seems kind of gross."

"Exactly this," she breathed after gulping down half. "It's not gross, it's amazing. Write down"—she waved a finger up and down—"whatever it is you just did to make this. I'll need more of it." She had another sip and grunted with satisfaction. "Okay, so. Do you remember who did the inspection when you finished the majority of the work? Just the stuff that has to be to code."

"Fred Geary."

"Cool. I'll shoot him a message tonight. Tomorrow we'll get rolling with paperwork and all that."

As she spoke she detoured from her circuit to walk to the front door, opened it to stick out her arm raised to the sky, and returned.

"Uh." She waggled her phone at Philip on her return. "They want to know if they can buy your furniture. Seems they really admire your style."

"The furniture? What— Like, how much of it?" Philip frowned. He understood, but still had trouble processing the request. Didn't they have their own? His wasn't anything special. "As in, along with the house?"

"Yep. I think they'll need to pay you separately, blah blah legal reasons, but they're interested in the patio set, the dining table, everything in here and the parlor, and the whole master bedroom suite. None of the smaller bits and pieces, though."

Philip looked all around. The leather chair he'd found at a flea market, the blue- and gray-toned modern sofa he'd traded photos for and otherwise couldn't afford, the light aluminum and planed barnwood table he'd made with Tom's dad, the church pew he'd salvaged as a bench by the front door. Lightweight and intricate rugs scattered on the hardwood floor he'd gathered, from the Middle East to South America. Everything he appreciated, and had chosen, but a bit strange seeming for someone else to want whole and outright.

"What about my houseplants?" He'd nurtured a veritable jungle that lived on high and open stacked shelves and stands along the two window walls. The jungle met thickly in the corner and was one of his favorite things.

Kelly pursed her lips. "Tom and I can keep them alive until you get resettled. My advice is throw in a pothos for the buyers, and if you're willing to part with the rest, ask high and don't bargain. If they can meet it, great, and if not you're not out anything."

"How much is a lot? Or not enough?" He imagined pretty high numbers. If he had to part with the house he could get mercenary.

"Are you willing to sell it?"

Most of what he owned he collected and acquired for this house. He'd never had anywhere to own stuff before that. College and then endless travel, a PO box to check between flights to wherever the next story would lead, a bed and a sink in a minuscule six-floor walkup he shared with some commercial pilot he'd never met. Before that— crippling poverty.

He'd built the bedroom set from slices of the huge tree that had to be felled before he moved in, figuring it out as he went. He had nowhere to take any of it, nothing to move it into. It might hurt less not to have it and start fresh, same as he'd done everywhere else.

"I'm willing."

"Great. Leave the asking price to me."

She disappeared into the front of the house again.

Philip made another cocoa peach thing and put it in a travel mug. "You've gone above and beyond for tonight. Take this." He blocked her from walking more and traded cups. "Let me see you to the car."

"Can I pee first?"

"Uh, of course."

"Awesome." Kelly shoved the travel mug right back into his free hand and hurried to the half bath he'd tucked under the stairs.

Philip brought the empty mug to the counter and then hovered, not wanting to seem like he was listening and waiting, but needing to be poised to stop Kelly from gaining momentum on resuming her pacing. They met in the hall and he propelled her toward the door, outside, and to her car.

Kelly accepted his help into the minivan, took the cocoa, and then patted the steering wheel. "Tom pretends to hate this thing, but if I could still fit in the Cooper, he'd drive it more than me."

"That I believe. He makes fun of me for having an all-wheel drive wagon and not a truck, but we both know he's gonna trade in the Mini for one like mine when the kiddo arrives."

She laughed. "Don't tell him, but I found a used one for sale at a lot a county over. I already contacted them and they're holding it. It's the same light green color as yours!"

"We can be twinsies," Philip quipped. The wind gusted and he shivered. He made a roll-down motion and shut the car door as she cranked the engine. "Thanks again for everything."

"Leave it to me. And you know we're glad to." She laid her hand on his, curved over the doorframe. "I'll text or make Tom text if there's any changes between now and the morning, all right? Otherwise come to the office because there's gonna be paperwork."

"Great, sounds good." He stepped back and shoved his hands into his pockets and watched until her taillights disappeared.

He glanced around to find the moon, a comforting touchstone no matter where he'd been, and located her not far above the trees mostly shrouded in clouds. He hurried inside, tossing his coat and hoodie on the couch, and knelt to the fire he kept laid. One match strike later it roared. Philip sat too close on the hearth as the stones warmed under him, and watched the flames and then worried he shouldn't have started it—but no, it was fine. Not like they'd move in tomorrow.

It was only that in the short span of coming to terms with everything having to change, everything *had* abruptly changed, and tomorrow he had to deal with that reality.

After he'd soaked in enough heat that his clothes were baked against his skin, he stood, stretched, and then wandered the house, turning off most the of the lights and staring too long into each room and all the furniture he'd actually cared to make or choose and would part with. He crept into his bedroom as if it was a trespass and traced tree rings in his—not his—headboard. The first bed that was only his.

Not a flophouse, not hostels on the trail of a story, not a cot or the ground under the sky or acrid smoke, the endless string of apartments and motel rooms and friends-of-friends' places he got dragged through growing up.

Well. At least he'd finally managed it. That had to count for something.

Philip rapped his knuckles on the solid wood, the varnish not yet mellowed by age, and then he snapped the bedside lamp off and kept going. At least this wasn't going to be drawn out. He couldn't afford drawn-out anyway.

When he got to his office, he caught the approach of something glinting between the trees and then watched the sweep of headlights creep past on the road. It wasn't as if there was never a random car on his quiet country lane, but disconcerting tingles skittered down his arms. He sensed it was *them*, checking out the house again. Making sure it was real. Anticipating.

He'd done so much of that himself it wasn't hard to recognize.

That and he just had a feeling.

He showered, hoping to wash some of that feeling and the day from him, got into comfy clothes, and drifted to the fireplace. He refused to dwell and using packing as a distraction seemed foolish until he had a list of what exactly they wanted, so he grabbed the book he'd tried to get into for the past month without much success.

Then he sat bolt upright and fumbled around for his phone to turn off the alarm.

He stared at it uncomprehendingly, rubbed his eyes until he saw sparks, and then got up to make coffee. As the pot warmed up, he pressed his phone to the front window over the sink and after a minute, it dinged a few times.

"Oof," he breathed and tried to work moisture to his tongue.

He yawned, yawned again, and then he widened his eyes and blinked until the spots cleared. He'd slept in far worse and less comfortable places, but he'd been younger and less beaten up then. Falling asleep in a chair wasn't kind to him anymore. He looked from the dying embers of the fire to the windows glazed with the coming dawn and shook his head. Having a house and a little routine had made him soft.

Philip grabbed his phone and took his coffee to the backyard. He watched small birds flit in the leaf litter at the tree line, and several noisy geese flew overhead. His mind spun to travel, something he hadn't done in a while. He couldn't believe it'd been months—a year—since he'd been overseas.

He could get right back into the go-go-go groove. Find things to cover in Nepal or maybe New Zealand. Or he could start small and finally get to Niagara Falls. Not quite the state line but he could cross into Canada. Make a run for Toronto. Hit the gas and not slow down or look back, figure out a reason for someone to pay him to do a story in Calgary and then Anchorage. Why not. He was free again.

Hand-to-mouth again.

He wished he'd chosen it, like when he'd determinedly left his mother and her addictions and mess behind. But he could still have it on his terms.

His alarm played again and he flicked it from Snooze to Off in annoyance. Then he remembered to read his text messages.

The buyers backed out.

House, furniture, everything.

Chapter Two

Philip moved a stack of knockoff Moleskines from one end of the table to the other. He fiddled with the twine he'd used to bundle them by the dozen and then the top one's ratty cover, still undecided about them.

For the past month he'd downsized even more, ruthlessly shedding the stuff that accumulates when someone stays still for too long, but he hadn't been able to pull the trigger on burning his old field notes.

On the one hand they didn't take up a lot of room and were the sum total of years of his life—his life's work. On the other hand, they took up room in boxes he had no plan to open anytime soon, given the supposed culmination of his life's work had stalled and ended.

He'd also sacked up and called Eric to talk about his book, and the lack thereof. Eric had been understanding and disappointed, had said vague but kind things about still wanting the book and being willing to get it back under contract, and encouraged him to keep the lines open and figure out a way to get past the blank void that had become his writing brain.

Between purging his sparse house and meandering walks, purposeful avoidance of dwelling on his mother's memory, hustling up work and the inane desire to get a cat, the blank void had only grown.

Philip sighed and patted the stack of notebooks. He left it and several more bundles there, undecided. If he could figure out other things to get rid of he could keep them, and the space he'd mentally allowed as reasonable in Tom's barn would stay the same. Other things he could dump without remorse. Other things had far less weight and no burden—a particular irony attached to stuff that felt impossible to shed.

Lunch would be a good idea. Driving into town to call around and try to sniff out some leads would be a good idea. Logical sense would be to combo that, but he couldn't afford to eat out. He could suck it up and head to Tom's office, get fed and use the internet. But he wasn't great for company these days, and he was weary of Tom's well-meaning suggestions and offers to help. Besides it was raining and he wasn't in the mood to get wet.

"Sandwich it is," he muttered and made another desultory PB&J that he washed down with the last cup from that morning's coffee. At least growing up less than poor and scraping by since made a no-frills approach second nature.

Since the astounding buy everything, buy nothing first day whirlwind, he'd had one other interested person. Nosy more like—a woman who wanted a look inside and get to gossip with Kelly about this long-abandoned place finally rescued. She'd driven away quite satisfied with herself, curiosity sated and for telling Philip what a nice job he'd done.

Kelly had screened a few similarly "interested" buyers after that, and none had made it as far as scheduling a private appointment.

Aside from personal stuff, and then daily needs like clothes and toiletries, there was very little left in the house. He lived in it as if on borrowed time, packing and repacking his belongings in smaller and more efficient ways, focused on repairs he'd previously been content to deal with until some nebulous later. That gave him something to do, and had the cold logic of the more he fixed, the more likely someone would want the house.

He'd sold some photo rights to image services and gigged some high school graduation photoshoots. He'd pulled puff pieces together from old material and submitted them to random online magazines. He'd tapped into his super emergency fund and even looked around town for jobs.

After the first would-be sale fell through, Philip had turned an imaginary hourglass. In a week the sand would run out and he'd be gone, no matter what, because there was nothing left to make up his growing shortfall and stay.

He thought he heard something and stopped chewing. After a long beat he definitely heard a knock, so he left the sandwich on the counter and took a swig from the sink tap to loosen the peanut butter from his teeth and answered the door.

A giant of a man loomed in the driveway, and it was something for Philip to think of anyone as giant, given he'd had Tom as comparison for so long. Tall, wide, fair-haired with clear gray eyes, in unscuffed work boots and worn jeans and a flannel over a straining blue T-shirt. But looming wasn't accurate. More, taking up a lot of space and cheerfully unaware of the effect or not self-conscious that he did.

Philip glanced around and took in the large but not tank-sized truck, the giant's relaxed demeanor and friendly nod, and the sun that had decided to appear from the clouds seemingly to shine just on this guy.

He closed the door behind him and walked slowly down the wide flagstone stairs that led to it, but stayed on the last one. Philip was six feet and with his whipcord strength and dark eyes could menace or seem taller, and had been glad of that during more than one tight spot. This guy met him eye-to-eye standing on the ground. Had to be about six-five, then, and casual clothes didn't hide rippling biceps and shoulders and linebacker breadth.

"Afternoon," the guy said with a crooked smile and an effortless stride to be suddenly standing next to him. He stuck out a hand and Philip felt all too keenly the heat from it.

Deep awareness rippled through Philip and he didn't dismiss or mind it, but he didn't need that, either. He kept his hands in his pockets and waited.

The guy finally withdrew his hand with a no-worries shrug. "Got it. So, if I have it correct, this house is still for sale? Your house?"

"Yes, it is."

"Nice, great. Okay, that's great. Well, I came by to talk about you needing to sell it."

Philip shook his head. "Ah, I see. I have a realtor but thank you all the same." He turned and made for the front door. He'd had more than one would-be hustle guy contact him about their winning ways to move the house, but none had gone so far as to make the pitch in person.

"I want to help you keep it."

That got Philip to turn back around.

He guy flattened a hand on his chest. "I'm Zak, Zak Springer. I was interested in your house before? I still am interested. And, if I accurately read between the lines of what Kelly explained, you don't really *want* to sell, it's more of a have-to-sell situation."

Philip ticked the name over in his mind until it clicked. "You and your… wife? You almost bought my house."

"That's right, that's me." Zak looked relieved and not the least sheepish.

"A month ago." Philip sounded flat, more unimpressed than angry. Normally the cold, damp air wrapping him in clamminess would have him showing them inside, but he didn't want to endure this chat in his cozy living room.

"Yeaaaah, that's—that's also right." Zak bit his lip and then tapped his chest. "And, she's not my wife."

"Girlfriend?"

"Not anymore."

Philip's eyes briefly widened. "Condolences?"

"Thanks, but it's all good. I think it was what famous people get to call an amicable split."

Philip didn't say more but Zak didn't budge or fidget or shift. His gaze did go to the house, following the angles and roofline and the curve of the front door, and the fondness lurking in his eyes almost had Philip changing his mind to invite him in.

"I looked online before I showed up to make sure the house is still for sale, and I hope we can talk about that. I have a proposal."

Philip said evenly, "I've changed my mind."

"You have? So you're staying?" Zak frowned as another idea seemed to percolate. "Do you live here alone? I got the sense you did."

"About the headboard."

"Headboard?" Zak's deepened frown etched into his brow but then the trace of a smile returned. "I don't follow."

Philip had said that to throw Zak off—to be mean because having to sell hurt. But Zak's only response was friendly, waiting for an explanation.

"See, I figure since you remember the house and your non-offer on it, you'd remember trying to buy all my furniture too. And I'm not interested in selling it anymore. At least not the bedroom set. And yes, I live here alone."

"I remember all of that. I'm who wanted all of that! That was part of the problem, but not the one we're discussing." Zak chuckled lightly and shook his head. "Whatever you've changed your mind about inside that's fine, like I said, I have a different offer now. But I am sorry the deal fell through. Honest. There were a lot more moving parts than I'd anticipated and they got the better of me, but I didn't mean to be a dick."

Philip's mouth pulled at the corner as his eyebrow went up.

Zak opened his hands. "There's nothing I can do other than saying sorry, that I mean it, and I did my best to stay away and save face. But here I am, because thinking about your place just got the better of me. And you don't have to hear me out, but I do think it's in your best interest."

"Oh, do you?" Philip sounded sharper than he intended but he didn't smooth it over.

"Like I said, it was clear from Kelly that you didn't want to sell but were motivated for reasons she didn't disclose. I can't blame you—your place is amazing." Zak looked around again and smiled. "I might have gotten my timing and understanding of my situation wrong before, but I don't think I'm wrong that you'd very much prefer to stay."

Philip didn't have a mouthy or a cutting rejoinder to that. Nor to Zak's sincere expression clearly hoping he'd give the slightest bit and listen. He made his hands open from fists and pulled them from his pockets. "I do need to sell, still."

"Okay, that's a start. See, I wanted to buy it because I have six months and a really important project to finish and then launch, and I thought getting some peace and quiet and nature would be a sweet setup to do it in."

"You'd buy a house just for six months?"

Zak laughed. "No, no. I'd live here for six months and then have it as a getaway after."

"How nice for you." Philip couldn't stay his bitterness at the blithe way Zak could consider spending thousands on a now-and-again thing. Hundreds of thousands. "I'm not seeing how this is good for me."

"I'm not explaining it well, that's why." Zak paused and then answered Philip's obvious, if unasked, prompt. "I'm getting there. Look, I was incredibly disappointed the sale fell through, which got me thinking about you being motivated—probably for the money, because you didn't actually want to go. Add in my six-month time frame, and...," he sounded out and leaned forward. "What if I rent the place? You can stay, you can travel, whatever suits you. I'd need like, a bedroom and a workspace, tops."

"There's no reliable cell service or internet."

It took Zak a moment but then he nodded. "Hey, that's cool. I need to limit distractions anyway. I can always run into town to send like, enormous files, or if the new season of my favorite show drops and I can't stand to wait."

Philip's insides buzzed and his thoughts raced, and he kept his expression and posture neutrally schooled. Six months was nothing, a blip, an easy span of days to be gone while this giant paid for him to get a second chance at keeping the house. He didn't like the idea of anyone else living there, touching his things, stealing a peace meant for him, but he hated the alternative more.

"When would this six-month stint start?"

"As soon as can be agreed, but it doesn't have to be tomorrow. Or the next day." Zak let that settle a minute and then added, "I'm prepared to pay upfront. Cash."

That flickered something in Philip he knew he couldn't fully hide. Confirmed when Zak's crooked grin showed again, a quicksilver of confidence and satisfaction.

"Can I think about it and get back to you?"

"No prob." Zak checked his watch. "You know what, I know. Meet me for dinner in town. My treat. We can hash out details—anything you want—and you can decide."

"Dinner?"

"Yes, dinner. You know, the meal you eat in the evening and is usually better shared with… someone." He'd obviously been about to say friends, but he and Philip were hardly more than strangers.

Philip considered that dinner someplace was better than hashing out details inside. Going to Tom's office and drawing up papers would be smarter, but something about Zak's eager friendliness and his own relief, that body heat he swore he could feel, made him agree.

He nodded.

"Great. Say around seven? I've heard good things about that farm-to-table place."

"You've heard good things because it's good." Philip nodded again. "Seven sounds fine."

"Perfect, thank you." Zak retreated to his truck, moving slow and easy. "Meet me outside and we can go from there."

"And if I don't?" Philip said for zero good reason other than he was terrible at friendliness and completely giving in.

"Well, then I'll eat alone. I hate eating alone, but I hate being hungry even more, and then I'll leave town and not return. Because I'll have your final answer on things, won't I."

"True enough."

Zak waited, but that's all the more Philip said. He stepped into the driver's seat that would present a bit of a climb for most other people, got the truck moving, but rolled to stop in front of Philip, arm out the open window and fingers moving shapes through the wet air. "Seven, at the restaurant, and I hope I see you." He thumped the quarter panel and then nodded and drove away.

Philip followed, well behind Zak's truck, walking the sloping curve of his driveway through budding trees and glacial leavings to the road. He texted Tom an invite to bring Kelly to the restaurant tonight and snag a table for four, and then without waiting for a response trudged back to the house.

He finished his dried-edges sandwich and packed the bundles of notebooks in a cedar chest that served as a coffee table. The blankets he kept in there could stay tossed on the furniture indefinitely. Then he walked to the back windows and contemplated the yard. Rent for six months to be in this specific house, to scratch the want that had surely itched since Zak had stood on the back patio? Philip wondered how much Zak would pay for that and just how mercenary he could get.

Dust and grime from the day's work necessitated a shower. He got into a pair of black jeans without any holes and tugged the better of his two sweaters over an ancient concert T-shirt. Then he loitered around the house until time to leave. The drive was easy and dark and he parked in front of Tom's office, because the restaurant across the square and over a block would be busy.

Zak stood on the sidewalk not quite in the short-but-evident line of the dinner crowd, unaware of Philip's approach, and that gave Philip the opportunity to scrutinize.

He was still handsome and huge, with a face more mobile and open as he watched the comings and goings from a slight remove. Everything he wore screamed expensive casual, long legs in fawn pants and a tawny fleece vest over a woodsy plaid shirt. His posture radiated physical competence, a sort of ready potential energy in shoulders and thighs, loose hands and wide-footed stance. He didn't look bored or anxious and wasn't scanning for Philip's arrival.

"Zak, evening," Philip said as he closed in.

"Hi. I'm glad you came." Zak's easy smile and a nod took the place of an offered handshake. He seemed even huger under the dim lights strung on the white and blue striped awning of Barb's Table than backdropped by forest and blue sky. His eyes seemed darker too, gorgeous and a kaleidoscope of grays and long-lashed and forget his size, they were the most compelling feature so far as Philip was concerned.

Philip checked his phone and then sidled past the line to the door. "C'mon."

It wasn't exactly cachet or a power move, but it was still satisfying to go right on in and lead Zak to a far back corner table where he saw Tom. As they approached, Tom's eyebrow shot up meaningfully, but he otherwise didn't react.

Zak detoured to the bar and had a word with Barb, of Barb's Table herself, and had her laughing after a brief exchange. He took bottles she handed to him and brought them to the table. Beer and raspberry lemonade.

Kelly had no filter left, so as they were getting seated she said in a quick jumble, "Gosh, it's Zak. Why did you bring Zak? Honey, this is the guy who was going to buy the house and then didn't. What are you doing still in town—back in town? How are you? Philip, I've been craving Barb's caramel bread pudding, how did you know!"

"Hello again, Kelly. It's great to see you. I'm doing good." Zak leaned in and brushed the air near her cheek with a kiss. He did extend a hand to Tom. "And you've got to be Tom—I'm Zak. Kelly talked so much about you, I feel like we're already introduced."

Tom had gone slack-jawed as he glanced between Philip and his wife. "Springer? Zak Springer was the would-be buyer? And no one thought to tell me this before, why?"

Philip flopped his hand open over his wrist in an eloquent *how should I know* gesture. Who was Zak Springer to him and for Tom to recognize?

"These two," Tom admonished, and half stood to grab Zak's hand in an enthusiastic vise. "How you doing these days, Heisman? How's the shift from left tackle field dominance to tech dominance treating you?"

Zak's eyes lit up and he measured Tom's almost-as-large proportions rising above the table. "Brother, I'm good. Go big D! What position?"

"Nose tackle." Tom snapped his finger from his nose straight out. "Right down the middle, eyes on the prize, baby."

Zak laughed. "Nice."

They launched into football speak and banter that Philip tuned out. He looked at Kelly, who had been with Tom long enough to parse and explain it. Philip cared about Tom, and that's as far as him knowing anything about football ever went.

Kelly lurched sideways on the bench seat toward him and planted her weight on her palm. "When he made the offer, I looked him up. His name was vaguely familiar to me, but I didn't immediately recognize the tech angle—he made his mark in the early days on some app with college friends. Wait, so you had no idea who he is?"

"I still don't." Philip waved his hands. "Why, should I?"

"He's a tech-made millionaire and prominent guru type, that's why. Aren't you supposed to—" Kelly gestured as if writing on a notepad with a pen. "—know stuff like this?"

Philip shook his head. "I'm a field reporter, not a tech desk guy. Journalists don't magically know everything."

"Say that again," Kelly snorted. She elbowed him and then said loud enough for the others to hear, "Zak also won the Heisman Trophy in college, and you know Tom loved playing, so it's the rules that they reminisce about glory days nostalgia."

Tom stopped midsentence. "Sweets, these are the glory days." He winked and his grin softened when she smiled. "But it is good to talk the game. Lawyers rehash the thrill of cleverly written briefs—I haven't run imaginary plays or been able to brag about a sneak tackle in years."

"It is good, isn't it?" Zak said as he handed out beers with the lemonade for Kelly. He held onto Philip's beer a moment longer. "I take it you'd like their input on my offer?"

Philip focused from having zoned out on watching the buttons down Zak's chest and abdomen almost gape as Zak moved and managed an even, "Yes, you take it correctly." He'd mostly wanted Tom and Kelly there to break up a tete-a-tete, but he tipped his head toward Tom. "He's my lawyer, so anything we come to terms on he'll need to know about anyway. I figured it made sense for us all to meet."

Zak nodded. "For sure, that's fine by me."

"Did you want to have another go at buying the house?" Tom's demeanor shifted from football buddy to attentive lawyer.

Through their friendship Tom had the insightful, kinda protective habit of asserting lead in various social situations, and Philip had the habit of letting him. He'd gotten Tom squeaked past more than a few guys wanting to fight or Tom being oblivious of brewing trouble, so he figured it evened out. He drank his beer and sat back, glad for Tom to break the ice but ready to cut in and hash out the details when they got to that.

"No, unfortunately." Zak pulled a rueful expression. "But it's not complicated. I need a quiet place to hunker down for a while, somewhere remote without being the back of beyond, just… out of the way of anyone being able to reach or get to me easily. This was already true last month, and I happened to be taking a meandering route to NYC from Toronto when an alert for a new property in the general area I'd hoped for popped up."

"Philip's property."

"Right."

Tom nodded. "And today?"

"Today I want to rent the house for around six months. We can get into why the sale fell through as soon as it materialized if anyone wants, but suffice to say I never lost interest and I hope this round will work out."

"He'd need the mortgage plus utilities and upkeep," Tom said without hesitation.

Zak paused, his gray eyes not as dark but not as open anymore either. He folded his big hands together on the tabletop and smiled. "I'm more than happy to pay more than what's fair."

"And you can more than afford it." Tom waited a beat and then chuckled, obviously pleased with everything. He clapped his hand on Philip's bicep and squeezed. "I see no reason to say no, and that's my advice as counsel and friend."

"That's encouraging." Philip looked at Tom, but his measured attention moved to and stayed on Zak. "I can let you know for certain in the morning." He would agree, he had to agree, but he couldn't give in quite yet.

"In the morning is perfect," Zak said over Tom starting to prod he just agree. "Can I put my number in your phone?"

Philip got his phone from his pocket and handed it over. He inexplicably—like a goddamn teenager—shivered when they touched. Zak's gaze flew to his and locked before wrenching away to study the phone. Zak's eyebrows furrowed, and Philip shoved his hand under his thigh.

Two large platters of appetizers arrived—fresh goat cheese and olives or dates, brussels sprouts in bacon and balsamic—and then flowed more beer and soon their dinners, winter squash ravioli, cabbage, and pork loin served family style. Barb didn't have a menu. Her offerings were eat what she made by the week or the day, and Philip was always glad to eat it.

Delicious food and alcohol, plus Tom and Zak's quick rapport, marked the end of any seeming need to talk about the house and all the factors they hadn't begun to figure out. Philip kept up conversation as necessary, but no more than that. He learned Zak hadn't played football since college, had that whole tech unicorn fortune thing going, and not a lot more.

He said very little, and even less about himself. Tom and Kelly didn't take it as anything other than the usual—even with friends Philip wasn't chatty.

Kelly returned to their table after her fourth trip to the bathroom and without sitting back down, bundled her coat over an arm and patted her belly. "I'm sorry, guys, but I'm beat. Even if I don't want to leave, the kiddo is about to make sure I fall asleep sitting here." She yawned and leaned against the wall.

"How about I take you home?" Zak folded his napkin onto the table and stood as he spoke before anyone else could move. "Philip, you know what you need to make it worth your while, Tom, you're here to advise him. And I need an answer." He zipped into his vest. "Is that acceptable to everyone?"

Tom looked to Philip to answer, clearly okay with Kelly snoozing on the drive to the farm with a fellow football warrior.

"If it's good with you two, I don't see why not," Philip said.

"Great. Go on and order dessert, get several even, and figure out what's best. We can connect in the morning."

"Dessert?" Kelly perked up through another yawn.

"How about we snag a pie or cake to go? Lady's choice," Zak promised.

"Then it's okay by me. And I think cake—the chocolate coconut." She grunted and moved enough so that Tom could stand and plant a kiss on her. "Night, Philip," she said as she went to study the dessert case.

"Remember, dinner's on me. Gentlemen," Zak said with an abbreviated bow and joined Kelly to get that cake and once again make Barb laugh.

Philip wasn't sure he had room for dessert but he'd order some. Maybe three. They'd be good to take home.

Low, rich laughter rumbled across the room and made his spine tingle and his ribs clench. Philip knew it was Zak and didn't allow himself to swivel in his chair to confirm or be able to watch when Zak laughed again.

"Ooh, interesting," Tom said lowly.

"What?" He tapped his fingers and pretended to consider something. "I'm thinking pecan sticky buns and carrot cake." Philip was good at concealing himself—everything—but Tom knew him too well.

"I'm thinking about my unerring sense that you like him."

Philip made a noncommittal noise. "I mean, he seems fine."

"Oh, fine, my ass. You *like* him, like him." Tom sat forward and jostled the table so their dishes clattered. "And aside from that, attractive and enormous and you've been a hermit for the past year and giving him sidelong glances about what I don't want to imagine and, oh yeah, enormously your type."

"Hey you know, fuck you," he said without heat.

"I'm always flattered when you say that, genuinely. But we agreed never to ruin our friendship over a quickie, and that promise meant something to me. It still does."

Philip dropped his head forward and laughed. Part of why he liked and trusted Tom so much was because there wasn't anything *but* abiding friendship between them. Tom had never been interested or acted weird about things; he'd never gotten drunk and slurred about being cool with accepting a blowie if Philip really wanted to.

"No one else would have noticed those sidelongs, so you're cool." Tom grabbed the last roll everyone had politely left in the basket, cut it in two, and thickly smeared it with butter. He handed half to Philip. "Are you actually into him? That wouldn't be a bad thing."

"Maybe I'm trying to get the measure of a guy I'm going to entrust my house to for six months." Philip honestly hadn't realized how much attention he'd given to Zak but Tom wasn't wrong. He'd paid attention to a lot of things about Zak—too many things. "Bad or good it doesn't matter. I won't be there." He tugged his beer closer as he slouched back into the chair and worked not to watch Zak leave.

"Add to your measurements he's nice enough to drop Kelly home so we could stay for a few beers."

Philip pulled his lips wryly. "Speaking of sidelong appreciation— you guys got along famously. He's real *nice* all-around it seems."

"He is, actually." Tom motioned their waiter for another round and planted his elbows on the table. "Look, I get that your credo is 'I trust three people and you're not one of them,' but I'm going with that's not the best way to treat the guy who's gonna bail you out." He leveled a stare at Philip. "Who you just might live with."

"If I stay put while he's there. If I agree." Philip picked at the corner of the label on his nearly empty bottle.

"Oh, c'mon. You're going to agree, that much is clear. You only made extra work for yourself having to call Zak in the morning about it." Tom moved when their drinks arrived. "Thanks, bud." He had a long swig and then nodded at the older woman behind the scrubbed counter that ran the length of the restaurant, separating the cozy dining from the bustling kitchen. "Zak even had Barb charmed, and she thinks if your great-grandparents weren't born here you're an outsider, and often treats you like one."

"Like I said—super-duper nice."

"Grudge it all you want, but I figure that's in your favor either way, the two of you together in the house or you giving him run of the place." Tom belched lowly and stroked his beard. "You got another gig lined up?"

Philip didn't, but he'd put feelers out. "Nothing solid yet but there's a few things I could go chase down. There's always something to chase down—I can simply go find it myself. Not like going back to being a stringer is beneath me. I have options."

"Options like sticking around and making another friend maybe." Tom waggled his eyebrows.

They were interrupted before Philip could answer he had plenty friends enough, thanks.

"Hi! Hi, sorry, sorry," Zak called as he nimbly sprinted through the restaurant to their table. He lowered into a crouch, searched the bench seat, and straightened with a triumphant grin. "Kelly forgot this," he said and held her phone out, recognizable in its pink-glitter case.

"Nice of you to come back for it," Tom said, shooting a look at Philip as he emphasized nice.

"Glad to, it's really no big deal. We weren't even out of town yet." Zak continued to be effortless, at ease, already comfortable in this locals-only establishment and in his own skin.

Philip pretended he didn't resent that. He wasn't and hadn't ever been easy, anywhere. Growing up as he did, he'd learned how to fit in the cracks, in the spaces people didn't notice or couldn't find, but he'd never been good at fitting in.

Zak opened and then closed his mouth, stopping whatever something chatty he'd had in mind to say. "Okay, I'm gone. Pretend I was never here. Back to—" He gestured over the table. "—whatever you were discussing. And don't forget dessert."

This time Philip did watch Zak leave and told himself it was his photographer's dispassionate eye that appreciated Zak's strong legs and incredibly *nice* ass poured into faded but expensive blue jeans.

Tom propped his cheek in his hand. "He's cute."

Philip grunted.

"And we've established he's your type."

Philip went back to picking at the bottle label.

"And he's so nice."

"And he's so straight," Philip fired back.

"You don't know that for sure."

Philip widened his eyes. "Trust me, I'm sure. He's sure of thinking he is, at least. That's obvious."

"And never stopped you in college."

"No, but I have far less tolerance for bullshit than I did back then."

Tom hooted. "Man, you've never had tolerance for bullshit."

Philip sighed. "You know what I mean."

"That you had more energy to burn chasing the slim prospect of getting some tail? Because sure, that I'll agree with."

"Got me there."

Tom clinked his bottle against Philip's. "You even managed it, a time or two."

"Eh, a few," Philip said under his breath, and his tension uncoiled when Tom barked out a loud laugh.

"What, are you being humble or something? You were notorious for cracking straight boys."

"Notorious?" Philip shook his head. "It's somewhere between humble and exaggeration, how about that?"

Tom made an agreeing noise. "I usually got a sense before all of them too. Just saying."

"You just say a lot. Too much." Philip spread his hands. "If you play it right, guys who think they're totally straight are a good, uncomplicated lay—if they admit they're interested. Getting to that admission is the tricky part. Makes for a bit of a challenge, you know. But after that, they're eager and horny and then just when I've had about all I want, they want to leave and go find something stable and reassuring like a girlfriend or a wife. It's good to mix things up from other types of guys not looking for any commitment." He shrugged unapologetically. "And all of that works fine by me."

"And if you don't do it right?"

Philip thought about Zak for a second too long. Thought about Zak in that context and didn't really like it. "You don't do anything."

"Easier said."

"And done, thank you very much."

Tom looked thoughtful and a touch mischievous. "Just maybe he'll challenge you."

That gave Philip pause. But he didn't dwell in it.

"Unlikely. Not because it's beyond my combined powers of persuasion and attraction, mind—you did point out I have no need to be humble." He leaned toward Tom and waggled an eyebrow until that baited the laughing groan he wanted. "I already resent he's going to live in my house, but I can't let that burn me up and be a complete ogre to him or get messy with mixed signals and whatever. Pleasantly neutral it is and will stay."

"Well, I'll give that you're a champ at that one too. I'd say it's more kind-of-civil neutral most times, but I get the gist."

"Well, I'll have you know civil and neutral has gotten me out of a lot of scrapes, mister big friendly talkative never met a stranger guy."

Tom beamed at the description and preened his mustache and beard down.

Philip waved a hand. "This six months has to be as uncomplicated as possible—after everything that got me here, I need that. And uncomplicated is almost no thoughts about Zak at all, in any respect."

He nodded like that settled it and then he kept right on thinking about how he could persuade and attract and where those combined forces would end. He cleared his throat and pushed those too-vivid ideas to a far and shadowed compartment of his mind.

"But yes, you're right and yes, I'll call him in the morning. I won't refuse the offer from stubborn spite. We've done plenty of dumb shit in life, but I'm not an idiot."

"We?" Tom razzed. He lifted his chin. "I get a good vibe off Zak and there were never rumors of anything awful about him as a player, and if someone's a brute or an asshole, it usually shows on the field. You hear things. He'll respect the house and your space. It'd be so good for you to get a grace period and recover, get your book back on track or go take some pictures you can charge a lot for and stuff."

With the top layer of paper gone, Philip moved onto the label glue, removing it methodically using his fingernail in tiny swipes.

"Not gonna sling yogurt at or share a bathroom with strangers, huh?" Tom's eyes twinkled.

"Man, shut up." Philip let out a short breath. "Hardly the same. Besides, like I said, I probably won't even be there."

"Right. Like you said." Tom nudged Philip's phone. "So—why not call now and let him know—if nothing else, you have reliable service sitting here. At least text? That boy's got some planning to do and not long to work with. Unless you want to keep being a jerk about it."

"Since when do you care about if I act like a jerk?" It shouldn't bother him but he bristled. "And I'm not a jerk, I'm just…."

"Knocked around by life, lessons hard learned, and made you careful. At best. I know." Tom pushed Philip's phone closer. "Even if you'd never admit it. Now, I'm going to go get us dessert so we can crunch this agreement into shape. A lot of it."

Philip grumbled and tapped his phone awake.

Hey it's Philip, just wanted to let you know that… he deleted. *Philip here, thanks for taking the time to meet with me longer to discuss…* he deleted.

Yes, agreed. Arrive anytime on Sunday, I'll be up early.

It took him far too long, and then a few minutes more, to send that. Then he dropped his phone onto the chair next to him so he could ignore it, lifted his bottle to acknowledge Tom's wise pushiness winning out, and downed his beer.

Chapter Three

Philip eyed Zak's duffel bag and backpack. "That's it?"

"It's plenty." Zak raised an eyebrow. "Assuming there's laundry here or a laundromat in town and a place to buy toiletries and such."

Philip traveled with less and never found it lacking, but he'd let himself anticipate Zak being fussier, even spoiled, and ready to take up a lot of space. Two tidy bags was incongruous to that, but the house already felt smaller and Zak was only in the foyer.

"There's shops in town and then a big box place about thirty minutes away." Philip motioned Zak in and closed the door. He considered how to proceed. Getting Zak quickly settled and them out of each other's way was what he wanted. "You know the layout so—let's get your things upstairs in a room."

Zak trudged agreeably after him. "Should I have brought linens? It's no problem for me to go get some towels and sheets."

"No, I have enough. Just plan accordingly with the sheets—I have one set per bed, so it's wash and remake same day. Or else you're stuck sleeping on a blanket."

"Right, got it. That'll be no problem."

Philip stopped at the top of the stairs and watched Zak's climb, slow and steady to take in the beech wood banister and listen to the creak of the treads and study all of Philip's pictures on the wall.

"Kelly said you're a photographer. Are these yours?" Zak paused on a step in front of one. The crumbled façade of a cathedral, rubble a blast zone all around it, and in the center of everything a cypress tree that had somehow been left unscathed.

"Most of them, yep. A few are prints given to me by colleagues." As he said it he noticed he didn't say friends, and it was strange to notice. But accurate.

"They're good. Wow," Zak breathed as he turned to look at the picture hung across from the fallen cathedral.

Dawn breaking over a wide landscape, gorgeous in color and low-huddled plants, but if you paid attention, the waterline lapping the beach was nothing but plastic trash, made soft and innocuous by the pretty light. Most tended not to notice.

Zak winced. "I hate this—what an amazing picture, and I hate it."

"It's grim. And thanks, that's what I was going for."

"You nailed it." Zak got closer to an intricately dynamic photo—an injured man carrying a child in one arm and pulling another along with his hand, the three of them cloaked in ash, dwarfed and menaced by a roaring conflagration in one half of the frame, and in the other half, the strange and stark break into blue sky and sun dappling a slope covered in bright blue-roofed buildings. He gently tapped the glass with a knuckle. "It's familiar but I can't quite place it."

Zak didn't look to or ask Philip for an explanation, so Philip didn't volunteer any. That particular photo had become the centerpiece image to tell the story of uncontrolled wildfires in a country far from the stairway and quiet house and surrounding wood. It being familiar to Zak without a specific memory didn't surprise Philip. A lot of his photos were that way for people.

Despite his pleasantly neutral strategy, buzzy appreciation played through him that Zak had noticed and taken such time with his photos. He put effort into his work, hoped always to transport and transcend, and shared it for reasons beyond a paycheck. Zak taking time with it— noticing—was gratifying.

"This one's different." Zak tilted his head at the smallest picture on the wall, nothing more than a candid 35mm taken with a run-of-the-mill camera. "It's stark, and more intimate than the rest. And makes me feel like I should know her but also that I'm intruding somehow." He turned to Philip. "It's a great portrait."

"Thank you." That was among the first serious photos he'd taken, using his grandfather's beat-up film camera, and it both showed and hid what his life had been like back then. He'd overexposed the shot—a mistake—but the end result was perfect. A fragile, finely boned woman and her laconic expression and gouged collar bones and tired eyes, summer dress caught in her legs and the cigarette she held between two fingers all hazing into the halo around her made by the too-bright sky.

Zak had another look. "She's beautiful, and I'm not convinced she's real."

"She was—beautiful and real. That's my mother."

"Was? Oh, I'm sorry about that."

"It's fine." Philip smiled lightly because it was, and because Zak had meant it.

The stairs ended abruptly at the second story, so Philip moved aside as Zak joined him in the open hall of bare and wide mellow black walnut floorboards. To the left was the master bedroom, as big as the kitchen and dining area, with big windows overlooking the backyard. To the right was the guest bed and cubicle bath, and straight on from the steps, his desk tucked into the eaves.

Philip turned left and reached behind him open-handed intent to take a bag.

"Hey, no, I plan to stay in the guest room. Much as I like everything about your room, as you know too well." Zak stayed put in the hall even after Philip crossed the threshold.

"Sure, but this room is better suited to you. I mean, it's the one bed you'll fit in."

Zak peered past Philip to the bed. His gray eyes warmed as his gaze drifted back and contoured across Philip. "I think you'll find I fit real well almost anywhere. I'm adaptable."

Philip's skin prickled delicately and he wasn't fully sure why. He resisted shifting or looking away from Zak. "Maybe, but you're paying a premium to stay here."

"And you own here," Zak said, matter of fact. He spun on his heels and walked to the guest room to close the argument. "I've slept on school bus benches and doubled with smelly football guys and tanked out in airplane seats built to comfortably accommodate hamsters. Trust me, this room will be great." He tossed his bags through the open door and grinned. "Good, that's settled. How about some breakfast?"

When Philip had agreed with Zak's suggestion the six months could start a week from their dinner, he hadn't expected to start coffee at seven in the morning the day of Zak's arrival and glance outside to see Zak's truck parked in the drive.

Tom had drawn up a simple contract. Three months upfront well above his actual mortgage rate plus a generous amount to cover the coming utilities. Not minutes after Zak had transferred funds, he'd paid every bill and breathed easier for the first time in too long.

"I eat breakfast." Philip started down the stairs and said, "You're welcome to use my room when I'm gone for work. It is actually more comfortable and wouldn't be an issue."

Zak's measured step was controlled, firm more than heavy, the width of his shoulders an inch from threatening Philip's framed photos, and he had to bend sideways to clear the soffit wall capping the narrow stairway. There was just enough headroom for him to pass through the low foyer, but once in the main part of the house under the high, sweeping ceiling, he didn't have to navigate quite as carefully.

Philip got his container of weekly oatmeal out of the fridge and a spoon from the drawer, set down a bowl and pried open the lid, and started to cut a gelatinous hunk loose. He lifted the container to get a gravity assist and let the hunk tumble into the bowl.

Zak watched on with raised eyebrows.

"I also have bread and a few eggs, but this is what I eat. It's slow cook so I make a lot in advance, as that's easier," he said diffidently. "Throw a little milk on it and it warms up fine."

"Sounds good—I'm all about batch cooking and honestly I love oatmeal for any meal. Especially with brown sugar and raisins." Zak moved in and pressed his thighs against the bar so it pulled his hips tilted forward, and flattened his palms on the counter, long arms locked at the elbows.

Philip stared at Zak's position, the prominence of bone and flare of muscles and leashed strength, blinked, and then turned to shove the oatmeal in the microwave. "No raisins I'm afraid, but I do have some brown sugar."

"But I actually meant 'how about breakfast' as in we go get some eggs and pastries and whatever, not make you feed me." He shrugged. "I'd planned to go shopping and stock the kitchen and get shower gel and whatever, and had thought… maybe you'd want to join me."

Unforgivably Philip very much did. "I can't," he said. "I have a lot of work to sort through and decide about, things I'd put off until I got the house situation righted."

"Cool, no worries. That makes sense." Zak smiled and stepped back, clearly not the least disappointed. "I'm going to stick to the stores in town so if there's anything I can grab for you, let me know."

His easy acceptance of Philip's rejection definitely didn't rankle Philip—for sure didn't.

"I use the basic stuff for the basics," Philip explained and crossed the kitchen to the wall that encased the stairway. He pressed the upper corner of a panel so it went in and then clicked open to reveal a washer and some bare shelves. "Just this, and this," he said as he popped his hand on the box of detergent and then a folded drying rack.

Zak loomed in behind him and snagged the detergent. "Earth-friendly stuff, got it. And we only ever had a clothesline growing up, so that's not hard." He nodded and was friendly and radiating body heat and way, way too close. "Are you leaving soon?"

"What?"

"Traveling—for work? I figured since you mentioned it upstairs something was pending."

"Oh." Philip licked his lips. Had Zak tracked the movement or was that his imagination? He licked them again and Zak's attention definitely strayed, and stayed, there. Could be promising, in the worst way.

Zak's eyes swirled with things Philip thought he could parse. Some awareness, mild confusion, interest, and then a rapid succession of thoughts. Those Philip couldn't know, but when Zak's brow hunched into a frown, he turned his shoulders and eased back into the kitchen.

The microwave beeped and Philip got his oatmeal. "I think probably so. That's part of what I have to get sorted."

"Any idea where to?" Zak's confusion and frown cleared but traces of pique remained, in the somewhat tenser hold of his body, and his gaze that followed Philip's movements.

"Too many possibilities to say just yet." Philip stirred the oatmeal and hid a grimace that he'd forgotten milk and that made it denser and gloopier than he preferred. He held the bowl under the tap and added water and then stirred until it thinned some.

"I hope it's somewhere good. Somewhere with more pictures to capture like those." Zak pointed in the direction of the stairs above them. He watched Philip a minute more and then shook his head, turned and tidied the laundry and closed the panel, and headed for the front. "You never said—do you need anything?"

Too much, Philip thought, taking in Zak's whole person and casual charm and wondering if six months would be enough to figure his finances and shit out and about six months of togetherness and where he could find to bolt to instead.

"Nope, all good. But there's some reusable bags in the back seat of my car—feel free to make use." He shoveled in a bite of oatmeal and nodded as he made for the dining area. He usually sat on the couch or stood on the back porch but even with Zak about to leave, it felt like company was around, so he sat at the table.

"Sweet, thanks. Back later," Zak called and then he was gone.

Hours later had Philip wondering where Zak was and distracting himself by working on the back patio. He'd collected rocks from the property and while on walks, and Tom had helped him clamber down to the river and basket-pull materials back up. He planned to soften the existing rectangle into the yard with undulating native plant beds and adding a stone path to the little lookout perch he'd created just from the wear of standing there too often.

But at the moment his focus of concern was a not-quite boulder of a rock he couldn't get to budge on his own, warring with his won't-beat-me stubbornness to get it where he wanted. He hunkered way down and planted his feet and lifted it about an inch, and it toppled in the wrong direction when he tried to give it a heave sideways.

He straightened and let out a long breath. Before he did something dumb he took off his gloves, threw them on the damn heavy rock, and walked away.

Philip snagged his water bottle and took the enforced pause as an excuse to stroll down the driveway to the road and check his phone. There might be leads on a job or a ready job to take, or maybe Tom needed something. Or a text from Zak checking in, which was what he actually wanted to find.

Nothing.

He walked along the road until another signal bar appeared and still nothing. Philip stopped, gulped the water bottle dry, and started for home.

The hum of an approaching engine made his heart thump in anticipation but he moved well into the verge because he couldn't be sure who it was. He resisted an unaccountable grin when the hum slowed and then kept pace with him.

"Well hey, stranger—need a lift?" Zak asked in a goofy-seductive voice.

Philip bit his lip to keep fighting that grin. "That depends on where you're headed."

"I think I can go your way, regardless." Zak leaned to pop the passenger door open and patted the seat.

He climbed in and grabbed the seat belt, and he tugged but it wouldn't budge. Zak reached past him, warm big hand grazing his neck, and then dragging down his torso to his hip and staying there, staying there turning from warm to hot, sensation frustratingly light yet too close to everything.

"There," Zak said as the lock clicked. "It sticks sometimes and ah… the angle can be tricky." Zak's hand loosened so his knuckles pressed into Philip as his fingers flexed.

Philip had forgotten all about his hand, and he remembered it after he'd wrapped his fingers around Zak's wrist. They stayed, motionless, for too long. Then Zak rolled his shoulders in a twitchy little shake, bolted forward in his seat and resettled, and then eased the truck into motion. Philip stared out the window and tried not to feel the burning lines Zak had traced into his side.

"Were you out on a run?"

"Nope. I've been doing some yard work and got mad at a big rock, so I took a break to check my phone."

"I see. What kind of yard work? Do I need to have a word with this rock?"

"You know, maybe so. I certainly wasn't convincing it of anything." Philip put both hands on the heating vent and then watched Zak thumb the fan speed and temp higher. He'd cooled down too fast and his sweaty clothes chilled him. "I want to add pollinator beds and expand the dimensions of the patio, but to be more organic in shape."

"Nice, I love that kind of project. Landscaping and the pollinator part." He paused. "The patio—that's a good spot."

Philip did finally smile. "Yes, it is."

The truck jostled as they turned into the driveway and Philip twisted in the seat at the distinct sound of a container of liquid thumping and falling over. His reusable bags had not been nearly enough, and he didn't usually need them all. Paper bags and packages filled the space behind their seats. More bags were snugged into boxes in the bed of the truck.

"Damn, what, did you buy the whole store?"

Zak eased the truck into Park. "I broke the first rule of food shopping—I went in hungry." His rueful expression bent crookedly, and he licked the corner of his lips. "The half-dozen pastries I got at the bakery only seemed to make it worse. But everything looked so delicious I couldn't help myself." He caught Philip's gaze and his tongue poked a bit farther out; then he dragged it in between his teeth.

"Risky, very risky." Philip's breath shallowed into his belly but he controlled the response to Zak's inadvertent display. "But I'll bet your food rampage made everyone's day. And their weekly bottom line." He exited the truck and figured out how to fold the seat forward. "That also apparently made you forget I have a small fridge and not many cabinets."

"No, that I did remember. And that they're virtually empty."

"Touché." Philip loaded two bags in the bend of his left arm and grabbed a third. He held that bag to his chest and managed to get the front door open, deposited them all on the counter, and got another load. They needed four trips each to get everything brought in.

"I appreciate the assist," Zak said as he emptied a bag and then neatly folded and added it to the growing stack. "You're welcome to anything I got—I saw they had the paper coffee pods for your machine so I got a variety of those. And there's beer and hard cider and sandwich stuff and good cheese and yogurt."

Philip snorted—muted, but still a snort.

"Not a yogurt fan?"

"I like yogurt fine." Philip hefted said yogurt and spun it against his palm to see it was the pricey French variety, plain. "I bet this is tasty with granola and berries."

Zak brightened. "I got granola, and berries! And, well." He glanced around. "Obviously plenty of other stuff. I hope you help yourself to whatever looks good. Where do you want all of it?"

"Seeing as I don't have much, wherever you want."

"Works for me." Zak began emptying things onto the counter. "And hey look, I got oats," he said as he tossed a package of oatmeal from a bag into his other hand. "Sultanas, raisins, raw and brown sugar, and some raspberry honey too."

Philip traced the writing on the tin of expensive steel-cut oats he never let himself buy.

"Anywhere, you're sure?" Zak had a cabinet open and a load of cans and jars pressed to his chest.

"Yep."

"Cool. I'll try and have it all make sense." He hummed abstractly as he moved around the kitchen, filling the cabinets with some order but low fuss.

Philip stood there making too intent a study of Zak's movements—big hands, quick hands, flex of arms and back and flanks—until Zak snagged the tin of oats from under his hold.

"I'll put this behind yours so we can find it easy." Zak looked over his shoulder at Philip and smiled. "Because that's your oatmeal I'm going to steal in the mornings. Or as a snack."

"That sounds… fine," Philip said to Zak's seeming to wait for a response. He'd been about to say nice, and then great, not fine. None of them were adequate to express liking that there was expensive oatmeal bought just for him and then happily stolen—shared.

"Take a pastry, I got plenty. They're still in one of the bags."

Philip peered into two and found it in the third, the hand-drawn sticker label of a bee flying over a loaf of bread slapped onto the tagboard box distinct from the premade grocery brands. He lifted it out and popped the lid. Zak had gotten at least three dozen goodies. Philip chose a bear claw and a lemon cream horn. He ate them too fast because he'd forgotten about lunch.

"I'm going to grab a shower," Philip said after loitering too long. It seemed awkward and maybe unnecessary to explain but he also didn't want to simply disappear. "Thanks for the pastries—and the oatmeal."

"My pleasure. There's not a lot better than a fully stocked kitchen. That's what my mom always says, at least." Zak closed a cabinet with satisfaction. "It feels true."

Philip didn't have a good answer to that beyond some noncommittal agreeing sounds. Most of his days he hadn't even had a kitchen. So he escaped to upstairs, stripped from his grimy clothes, and streaked into the bathroom.

He stayed in the shower far past what soaping up and rinsing required. The heat on his sore muscles was welcome, and the white noise quieted his mind. When he was pruney and pinked, he shut the tap and turned off the tankless water heater.

"I should show Zak how to do that," he muttered.

Philip scrubbed dry and held the towel at his waist and frowned at having completely blanked on fully closing the bathroom door, so during his shower it had eased wide open again.

"Tell me what?" Zak asked as Philip stepped into the hall.

Philip didn't startle. Nothing about that kind of weakness when young had been safe and fieldwork had inured against making any reaction. But goose bumps broke across his skin as he turned around and met Zak's gaze.

Zak was in the shadow of his doorway, holding a notebook and a tablet. "Sorry—I didn't mean to pounce. I heard my name and naturally responded, but I realize normal folk not raised with siblings and in locker rooms would have left it for later."

Philip let a little demon knot the towel almost too low and walk him to the bathroom. "I'll show you now."

Zak tossed his stuff down and crammed into the room after him.

Philip patted a boxy appliance fitted to the wall next to the shower. "I went with tankless water heaters in the house, but with these you have to turn the big silver dial when you want any. It's a European model— they're way more energy efficient and yet the hot water seems endless. I actually got the brand I used in a swank boutique hotel once."

"Swank boutique hotels don't strike me as your preferred means of travel."

"They're not. A legacy magazine put me up there while doing a story, back when legacy magazines did that kind of thing."

"You probably complained the whole time and couldn't wait to be in an unreliable Toyota crossing some desert chasing warlords or refugees again."

"That's…." Philip let out a short breath. "Painfully accurate."

"I enjoy rough camping too, but I can't say I've ever done it for anything more noble than good fishing or wanting to get under dark skies or tackle a long summit trail."

"It all has its place." Curiosity got the better of him. "Did you catch any fish? And what dark skies?"

"I'm a shit fisherman. My dad wasn't, though. He had the knack, and that's why I bother."

"Was? I'm sorry," Philip said, echoing their earlier conversation.

Zak nodded, and then his crooked grin flashed. "I should just admit I'm best at being a sit-by-a-river-quietly-for-hours guy. And the dark skies is anywhere I can find them—parks, islands, remote spots that feel forgotten. I just love it. I can close my eyes and still see the full moon, heck, a quarter moon, in a sky without light pollution."

"I know what you mean. I once managed to time a full moon in an aurora. That was incredible and the pictures I got are good, but they couldn't do it justice. The depth simply isn't there."

"I hope you'll show them to me."

Zak touched his arm to emphasize the ask and Philip shivered, not lightly like in the truck but deep in his gut and low in his groin.

"Dang, I'm gabbing at you and you're getting cold." Zak poked the water heater. "This dial you said?"

Philip nodded. Leave it to him to decide it imperative to resist the only person who'd ever made him crackle and ache, only just met and hardly sharing a touch, immediately and full.

"Well, since I'm in here." Zak turned the big silver dial and notched the temperature up and up. Then he grabbed the hem of his shirt and stripped in a fluid motion.

Philip got an eyeful of hard pecs and defined abs, cut hips and a tantalizing trail from Zak's belly button that disappeared under worn jeans. He let himself look.

His gaze tracked Zak's reach and kept skimming down to bare feet when Zak popped his jeans open. Nice feet, large and manicured with prominent tendons. Zak's big toe curled and grabbed his cuff and his pants dropped to puddle on the floor, no more nice feet in view. He managed to wrench his attention up when Zak's thumbs slipped into the designer label waistband to peel boxer-briefs away, but he couldn't move a muscle.

Zak blinked and then smiled. "When I'm finished we should have dinner. As in make and sit down to eat. Sound good?"

"That sounds fine." Philip didn't budge and Zak didn't move and steam began to billow around them, standing too close, nearly naked in a pillowy cocoon. He finally stepped back. "Since there's no window, I leave the door open a crack or it's steam city. That okay?"

"Perfectly."

Philip turned as Zak got into the shower and beat a retreat to his room. He left the light off, preferring the dim blues of twilight but also needing the cooling shroud it covered him with. He slathered on lotion and then stared out the window, breathing in, breathing out, until his pulse calmed.

He was well into chicken thighs and roasted potatoes—and wondering what he was doing going to any trouble while rationalizing that they had to eat and it might as well be decent—when Zak joined him.

"Smells delicious." Zak's honey-blond hair darker and slicked down with water was as appealing as lighter and teased by a breeze. The fitted and clingy damp T-shirt wasn't bad either.

"Salad or broccoli?" Philip asked from his study of the refrigerator.

"Both."

"Both it is."

Philip was accustomed to frozen florets and iceberg lettuce and dressing. Zak had gotten fresh bundles of broccoli and the gourmet salad kits the market put together.

"Wine?" Zak asked as he held up two bottles. "What are you making?"

"Chicken, potatoes. But nothing fancy."

"Not fancy is fantastic. I grew up eating nothing fancy and it served me fine. Hm, I think this Chardonnay should go well with that." Zak fished in a drawer for Philip's cheap corkscrew. He added in a snooty voice, "I'm told this is a very good one."

"So, something fancy after all."

"Oooh, indeed sir," Zak agreed in the goofy voice.

Philip laughed and shoved the broccoli and the salad kit onto the bar. He checked the meat and turned the potatoes, and Zak found a bowl and dealt with the salad and was chopping the broccoli before Philip got back to them.

He brought the salad to the table and Zak laid two place settings, using the stoneware pottery dishes Tom and Kelly had gotten him as his housewarming gift. Philip had, after that, mostly used his old, mismatched plate and bowl.

"Wineglasses?"

Philip poured avocado oil and seasonings on the broccoli and as he stirred, tapped the high and narrow cupboard above the range. He didn't move when Zak stepped in and reached over him.

Zak inhaled, almost sighed. "You smell good." He huffed lowly. "You didn't strike me as a boutique body cream guy, either."

A tickling sensation chased from Philip's scalp down to his tailbone. Zak's breath and body heat, almost overwhelming, and despite attempts he was unable to ignore the warmth generated by their proximity.

"I became one by necessity. With everywhere I knocked around I'd be leather otherwise, and I learned the hard way the cheap crap won't do."

"It's nice," Zak breathed and stood there a moment more.

When he stepped away it made Philip cold, made him want to chase Zak's heat.

The rest of dinner didn't take long to make. They worked well together, close and overlapping and busy, but never in each other's way. Zak hummed as he lit a candle and poured the wine and Philip blanked his imagination as he got the potatoes into something while Zak put the rest of the food on the table.

Zak refilled their wine, keeping them to linger at the table even with dinner eaten. "You're a damn good cook. That was all delicious."

"I get by. If you wanna eat, you learn to cook."

Zak made a thoughtful noise as if Philip had given something away. "My mom taught me and brothers and sister. We're all varying degrees of successful, but at least takeout isn't the only thing standing between me and starvation."

"Was she a good cook?"

"Amazing. And still is." Zak smiled fondly. "Of course, she said she's retired from cooking. Moved to New Mexico and got into book clubs and knit clubs and litter-gathering clubs instead. And she's become a cruise devotee."

"That doesn't sound too bad."

"According to her, it's living the dream." Zak fiddled with his wineglass. "That leaves your dad. Is he…?"

"I don't know."

Zak's thoughtful noise to that, as if Philip had given something more away, was because he had. A lot was conveyed in his compact, bald words.

They had more wine and Zak polished off the potatoes and then they sat in pleasant quiet.

Philip broke the silence. "What are you here to work on, if I may ask?"

"Another lightning in a bottle app concept."

"Any ideas?"

"Not a one." Zak shook his head.

"Hopefully something clicks."

"I set time aside, am here, and got a special notebook just for brainstorming. I'm halfway there." Zak smiled wryly and then leaned forward. "So, come to find out you happened to have won the Pulitzer at some point. How about that."

Philip didn't demur or boast. "It's opened some doors a bit wider."

"I told you that one photo upstairs was familiar, but I couldn't place it. And after that, I couldn't shake wanting to figure it out. So I snooped on Philip Conyers and first result, there it was. I didn't even have to dig." Zak shrugged one shoulder. "You didn't seem to want to talk about it, which I don't mind. I hope you don't mind I looked."

"Not at all, Mr. Heisman Trophy Winner, thanks to his incredible athletic abilities along with—what was it—diligence, perseverance, and hard work on and off the field. The picture of you accepting the award, all dressed up in your little suit. I'd have taken better, obviously, but you looked cute." Philip stopped short and would have grabbed the words out of the air and smothered them if he could.

"Mom picked out the tie, and the pocket square," Zak said without seeming worry or notice. He grinned. "It's good you snooped too because that makes it less weird for me, relieves me of any awkward guilt. And congratulations. A Pulitzer, wow."

"Back atcha," Philip said and grinned too easily back. After a moment of liking sitting there, grinning at each other in the light buzz of alcohol and good food and making each other laugh, he set his glass down with a distinct rap and started stacking dishes.

"Oh no you don't. The cook doesn't clean up. House rules."

"Are they?" he asked too sharply.

"Yeah! At least they should be—can be."

Philip walked his load to the sink. He turned and Zak had remained, standing by the table, looking uncertain for the first time since they'd met.

"Yeah then, okay. Whoever cooks doesn't have to clean, house rules."

"It's a good rule. Gran's and then ours, but really, I think it's almost everyone's."

Philip had almost no rules growing up, but he'd created several for himself in order to get by.

"Since you'll be busy, I'm headed on up. Work stuff and I need to get some reading done."

Zak already had the water running after cranking the tankless heater under the sink. He waved acknowledgment, and a glob of suds sailed from the end of his fingers to slap on the floor.

Philip paused at the photo that Zak had recognized enough to go hunting for info. It'd been early days for him, and the prize money had kept him afloat far ahead of the prize itself burnishing his career and prospects. Tom had talked him into putting a portion of the money in a market account, which he'd not quite drained as part of his determination to get this house. He was sure there were ironies or strands of fate in there, somewhere.

He peeped into the bathroom. Tidy, and sandalwood and lavender lingered in the air. He didn't know why he'd looked or what he'd expected to see. His phone propped in the windowsill over his desk pinged with several notifications, so he opened his laptop. There were emails to clear and a few to answer, and one or three jobs he'd have jumped at not long ago. Tough jobs, faraway jobs, jobs that sitting there listening to the dishes getting done and Zak's low, off-key singing made hard to want.

But he'd definitely consider them, which he said to each inquiry or filed as possible to go and run down.

He tried poking at his defunct book and writing was nothing, still nothing, so he stretched out in bed with the novel he'd been trying to read and then lay there, mind adrift, mostly staring at the wall.

Chapter Four

Philip slept poorly and woke early and repeated that the next several days.

He wasn't a morning person or a night owl. Life had lacked all structure for that, and he wasn't naturally inclined one way or the other. Mostly he slept in progressive rhythms, going from waking before dawn but staying up too late, which pushed his wake-up time later and later over the course of a few weeks, until he was getting up at ten and finding it hard to fall asleep, so he'd be up at dawn again.

House cohabitating was at one week, and it was far too comfortable and disturbing and Philip hadn't made any attempts to escape. They had oatmeal, Zak disappeared into town or went for runs and Philip went for walks, and then Zak would return. They'd wind up on the patio or the overlook together, and they worked more in the yard, getting so much accomplished they'd tackled more and then more with Zak's willing help and input.

Once cleaned up—and Philip wanting a repeat of their shower swap and Zak oblivious—he'd pretend to be busy with his laptop while also pretending he needed the room in front of the fire instead of the tiny nook at his desk while Zak lazed comfortably and wrote notes on something or read until they had dinner. Not even *hey do you want to eat* dinner but as an already established routine they'd slotted into since the first night.

Philip was up too early again and gritty-eyed. Yard work was his plan for the day. Zak had said last night that Sundays were for staying home, and wasn't that going to be great. Probably, and great in ways Philip didn't want to keep teasing himself with. But he could burn hours outside, and hours away from Zak seemed like the smart call.

He dressed in layers; the shade ahead of any sun would be too cold to face without a hoodie even though he'd warm quickly once he got going. Then he crept downstairs, used the bathroom, and got his gloves from where he'd dropped them yesterday.

The coffee maker was set to start in an hour and since he wasn't ready for any he left it, grabbed a cinnamon roll, and wolfed it down with a glass of water. One of his first projects had been fussing and tweaking the sliding door until it moved in virtual silence; easing it open in the quiet house, aware of Zak asleep upstairs, made him doubly glad he'd gone to that effort.

His tools were lined neatly against the house, and he considered the options and then chose the shovel.

Chopping out sod, breaking up soil, transplanting the native plants he'd gathered while on his walks and nursed in the shelter of the woods, and imagining how it'd look all grown and full of critters was meditative and satisfying. He'd done plenty of lawn care and maintenance through the years and never minded the work, but there was a big difference between tending someone else's manicured landscaping and digging in to create your own planned chaos.

"All right coach, put me in."

Zak's bright voice startled him. Catching him off guard—another way to already be under his skin—rankled. He hid that in splitting a clump of grass that would grow knee-height and bear tons of feathery, oat-like looking seeds. It occurred to him they'd mature in time for him to say to Zak look, more oats, and the fleeting thought was welcome.

He didn't know how long he'd been working but the sun had topped the trees.

Zak stood hands on hips, dressed in ready-to-get-grubby clothes. "First, though—cream or sugar or neither or both?"

Philip stared blankly.

"Coffee's ready and I poured two cups, but I don't know how you take it."

"Coffee sounds great. Both, and a lot."

"Can do."

Zak wasn't gone five minutes and Philip gratefully took a steaming mug.

He had a sip. "Perfect," he breathed.

"Super, I'll remember that." Zak stuffed a pair of work gloves into a pocket and had a long drink. "Actually, tell me all about what you're doing and then put me to work."

"You happened to have a pair of gloves?"

"Sure, I keep a pair in the truck. You never know."

Philip nodded and walked to the far end of the patio. He could say scram or assign a task in a whole different area, but foolish pleasure in Zak's company won out.

"I'm developing naturalized plantings to transition from the patio to the woods. So, where I've dug is sunny, same as all the edges of the pavers." He gestured with the shovel handle as he talked. "That'll be rocks that lift from the flat pavers into the terrain of grasses and flowers. Then I want to put shade plants in to blend into the trees," he said and stepped backward, drawing the leading edge of the bed he envisioned with his free hand. "Probably with more rocks."

"Always with more rocks." Zak narrowed his eyes at the stupid almost-boulder sitting in the middle of the yard. "Say like that one—that's a great rock."

"That asshole might stay there."

"Ahh, the one I'm supposed to have words with, got it." Zak laughed. "You look ready to fist-fight it."

"Well, it'd win."

Zak's laugh deepened. "We can best it, I know it." He sliced his hand up and down through the air. "Is that worn path going to be plants or a walkway?"

"Walkway, and then make all around it plants. Eventually." Philip crossed to the path and went to the overlook.

Before he could say anything, Zak had come to join him.

Zak whistled lowly. "Man, what a view. That's gorgeous."

Philip watched him take in—and notice—everything to be seen from the overlook. The almost horseshoe bend in the river to the near north and then straightening to cut at the bottom of the property, continuing on west while breaking gently south. Across the river the ancient rolling mountains lazed under the sky all covered in forest and bare spots of granite.

"All of that's a state forest," Philip explained and pointed from one compass end to the other.

"How awesome to know this will never be spoiled."

"It is. It's no good as graze or farmland so there's not a lot of demand for development, and sometimes the state does come through and cull usable timber, but that ain't too bad."

"No it ain't." Zak pulled in a long breath and held it. "When I came to the house the first time, I had no clue about all this. But I knew the place was special. Standing on the patio and looking at the sky, under the moon, you can tell. It's in the air, like. Here." He patted his chest in a sweetly unselfconscious gesture. "I have to make time to get down here for every sunset—they're spectacular."

Zak hipped into Philip and then remained, warm and solid against his side.

Philip didn't move. "Yeah. They ain't so bad either."

"An outdoor fireplace would be awesome here too, some comfy benches and oversized Adirondacks. Think of the peak coziness you could achieve in late fall with blankets and cocoa and s'mores."

"That sounds okay I guess." Philip wondered if he'd been too dry but Zak got him, and then matched his tone.

"I'd manage to endure an evening or two of that, somehow."

Standing there together finishing their coffee was definitely not bad.

After several minutes Zak tapped his foot on the hardpack ground. "Do you have more rock for this?"

"I'm working on that." Philip looked up at Zak. "Let's say I'm more foraging these projects than financing them."

Zak smiled. "Great approach. My dad and I managed more than a couple projects around the house I grew up in using that method. And it means you get exactly what belongs to where you relocate it, so it fits in just right."

"Yes, exactly." Philip chewed on his lip and turned back to the view. He didn't need to get too invested in any metaphors, standing with Zak like this.

Zak clapped once and rubbed his hands together. "I could stand here all day, but enough gawking. Let's go move the big daddy rock, and then you can show me what plants and things to keep an eye out for that we want to adopt." He gathered their mugs, nudged Philip sideways so they at last broke contact, and made for the patio.

Philip pulled his gloves on and got ready opposite the rock from Zak. "It's way too heavy to lift into the wheelbarrow, so I've been attempting to roll it into place. But I have a hard time getting that last push to change its momentum to going rather than falling back down." He pointed. "I used that bleached branch to mark the spot."

He wanted the large, pinkish and black-dappled rock to sit at the curving prominence of the longer sided bed, where the shade plants, the grasses, and what little he'd leave of the lawn would all meet.

Zak paced the distance. "About twenty feet, we can manage that no problem."

They absolutely could not.

Almost halfway to the goal had them panting and stretching uncomfortably, after attempting using ropes that didn't hold as a carry hammock, a side-to-side walk of the rock that nearly crushed Philip's foot, and then angry brute force that got them the farthest but also the most wrung out.

Zak winced when he straightened. "I haven't felt these muscles since football training camp." He huffed several long breaths and let his head fall back. "How'd you get it pulled this far from the woods in the first place?"

"Tom's ATV. We got a lot moved by dragging stuff around on an ancient sled and some chains. I told him where we left it was close enough—it seemed so at the time."

"What's he doing this very minute, do you think?" Zak hunkered again and braced his thighs. "I say we give it one more try, and then your grand vision is gonna have to change."

Philip eyed the rock. "I can't disagree. There's always more coneflowers but only so many good years left in me."

Zak snickered. "You push, I'll pull, and we can topple the pointy end that's sticking up but like, maneuver it so it doesn't just get wedged in the ground again. Simple as that, right?"

"Right, easy. No problem." Philip grimaced. "Shit like this always gets me with that whole 'one more try' thing."

"Me too." Zak grinned—a flash, crooked—and then got serious and nodded. "On three."

Philip made the count, "One, two, three!" and on three, he pushed and Zak pulled and the weight of the rock yanked him forward and flying to stumble over the rock and knock Zak down.

Zak yelped, and they instinctively rolled. They came to a stop, Philip pinned to the ground under Zak and the rock mere inches from his head.

"Death by stupid almost-boulder is not how I thought it would end." Philip covered his face with his hands and groaned, and then he started laughing. Frustration, the ridiculousness, the spike of effort and then near-miss surge of adrenaline.

Zak laughed too, against him, sat straddling his hips and still automatically checking him for injury. "But will you live?"

"I'll carry on, somehow." Philip let his arms flop open, and he squinted past Zak into the sky.

"Brave lad," Zak said in a whisper, and his smirk softened to something else entirely as he ran the length of Philip's loose arms with his hands until his palms were pressed flat to Philip's chest.

Philip swallowed. Well—this was cliché. And utterly appealing. He gazed up at Zak, flushed and surrounded by soft afternoon light. It stole his breath.

"Shit, I knocked the wind out of you. Sorry." Zak's pupils were dilated, and his gray eyes dark.

"I'll take that to being concussed by the beast." Philip moved to capture Zak's wrists, intending to get the two of them moving and separated, but all he could do was leave his thumbs over Zak's pulse point and skate his fingers across the top of Zak's hands. That pulse skipped a beat and sped, and the sensation, the tell, satisfied him in dangerous ways.

"Hey-o! Philip! Bud, are you around?"

Philip groaned and let his grip go and then fall. He raised an arm and waved at Tom. "Here, suffering, dying for my gardening sins."

He shook his head at Tom's grunty laugh.

Zak waved at Tom and stood in a fluid motion, easily hauling Philip up with him. "I'll go get us a drink," he said, not the least bothered or flustered.

Tom didn't comment but when Zak turned away, he waggled his brows suggestively.

"What's up?" Philip casually straightened his clothes. He was stupidly flustered, resented Tom's intrusion, and was very glad for it.

"Kelly sent me into town on a peach preserves mission, but it's out of season and the market doesn't have any. I'm throwing myself and my survival on your mercy."

"Sure, of course." Philip had his breath back—itched with the ghost sensations of Zak's weight and heat covering him—and he propped a foot on the stupid, stupid rock.

"Oh no, not that bitch." Tom scowled.

"So, you two have met before," Zak said as he returned with cans of sparkling water.

Philip took a mango lime something and drained it in one go.

"I have some unfortunate acquaintance with this beast." Tom set his unopened can down, tilted his head in study of the rock, and then pointed at the bleached branch. "You wanted it there?"

"Yup."

"Great. Let's get it moved where Philip wants it, once and for all. Even if I have to run home for the ATV. Then I can be a double hero on this day."

A lot of cursing, straining, grunts to yells so no one lost a limb, and leaving the rock about two feet shy of its destination got them there.

Philip sat on the ground, hard, and brought his knees to his chest.

"I am out of shape," Tom wheezed and plopped down next to him. "Humbled—by a damn rock."

Zak remained standing and ate a cinnamon twist. "It does look real good, though, even if it did shorten our lives." He winked at Philip. "You had the vision."

"And let's hope he stops seeing things after this. Ugh, ouch ouch nope, I'm locking up." Tom stretched and then pitched sideways to half climb the rock to his feet. "I'll bet you're about to freeze fast there, champ," he said to Philip and reached down.

Before he could grab hold, Zak had hold of Philip's elbow and then hip and then Philip mostly under his arm.

"We should do a slow walk so we don't cramp up later." Zak squeezed Philip's arm to start them moving.

Tom shot Philip a *well well well* expression that made Philip disentangle from Zak and slightly change direction. The three of them milled around until by silent agreement they met at the patio and stopped.

"Thanks, guys, obviously that wasn't going to get done on my own." Philip got his empty can and handed Tom the fresh seltzer. "And now, peach preserves." He went inside and left the sliding door open behind him.

"Soooooo," Tom said as he came into the kitchen. "How's things with the roomie?" He shot a glance at Zak on the patio doing some obscenely low lunges and hammy stretches and looked back to Philip.

"Everything is going fine so far, but it's not like he's been here long enough to get on my nerves."

"People who are going to get on your nerves do so within five minutes and once that's established, you never forgive them for it." Tom looked to Zak again. "A few days and you're rolling around in the yard laughing with the guy? I'm just saying."

"Why are we friends again?" Philip found the preserves in the fridge and held out the jar.

"How much time you got? I can go get my list of amazing qualities from the car, if you want a refresher."

"I think I know what you can do with that list."

Tom snickered and Philip set the jar on the counter just beyond Tom's reach.

"Wait, did I hear there's a list?" Zak strode in and did that very distracting hips-pressed pose against the bar counter.

Philip widened his eyes in exasperation at Tom for noticing his distraction.

Tom grinned. "The list is what I suggested we have for early dinner at my place. After exerting dominance out there, we need to celebrate man's victory over nature with some grilled meat and cold beers."

"More like needing to nurse our war wounds," Philip muttered.

"That sounds great, actually. Can Philip and I clean up first and head over in say, an hour?"

"An hour or so would be perfect. I'll get the grill fired up and we'll be waiting." Tom walked through the house toward the front door, stopped, and took the jar he'd forgotten from Philip. "Zak, how do you like your steaks?"

"Medium rare."

"That's just how Philip likes it too," Tom said expansively and smirked at Philip.

"Is it?" Zak nodded agreeably and wound up standing on the top step alongside Philip. "Can we bring anything?"

"Just yourselves." Tom's smirk bent almost evilly as he glanced from Philip to Zak and back. He got in the car and tooted the horn halfway down the driveway.

Zak sort of ushered Philip inside. "Do you want first dibs at the shower? I only need a quick rinse."

"Go on ahead, I need to get everything put away in the back."

They parted in the foyer and he discovered there wasn't much to do, as Zak had obviously gathered and stowed everything neatly as he'd talked with Tom. God, what was with this guy—thoughtful, considerate, *nice*. How irritating.

Philip stayed on the patio for a bit staring at the overlook, thinking about s'mores. He huffed, straightened his shoulders on the way back in, and slammed and locked the sliding door.

"You back in? I'm all done," Zak called from upstairs.

It didn't take Philip any longer to get cleaned up and changed into just a little more than his usual. Ass-looks-good carpenter pants, black long-sleeved shirt that fit tight, and a mossy toned flannel with only a few buttons done up.

"Ready? I'm ready." Zak rose from the bench in the foyer as Philip descended the stairs, gaze flicking from the pants to the hint of Philip's torso and back. He wore jeans and a goldenrod cabled sweater with the peek of a green shirt underneath.

"Just about." Philip grabbed his wallet and phone and a tube of lip balm from the wood-turned bowl on the nearby credenza. He got each item shoved into a pocket and then nodded.

Something about their complementary little actions, the almost routine of the day, of getting in the truck and settling in felt good. They rode in silence through town, Philip painfully aware of how good Zak smelled and how he'd used more lotion than usual because Zak liked the scent.

Zak slowed way down and parked parallel to the bakery. "Favorite cake?"

"Cheesecake."

"Huh, okay. I guess that counts." Zak popped the door and slid effortlessly to his feet. "I won't be a minute." He was back in under three and held out a box as he climbed into the truck. "Could you take this?"

Their hands met and Philip repressed irritation at the electric jolt that passed between them. The silence in the truck changed then, ratcheted into light tension, but it wasn't exactly bad. Still, Philip was relieved when they got to the farm.

"Hail the conquering heroes," Kelly said as they let themselves into the house.

"Hiya, Kel," he said and gave her a sideways hug.

"Thanks for coming in clutch on the peach stuff." She tilted her cheek toward Zak.

"You're looking radiant as always," Zak said and gave her a quick peck. He motioned at the box Philip held. "I know Tom said not to bring anything, but we got dessert."

"Dessert? Nobody here likes that. I'd better just hide this away until I can dispose of it." Tom took the box and led them into the kitchen, showed off the steaks and sides he'd prepped, and then gave them beers. "G'on in and sit down."

Everyone did, and then everyone got up and checked the grill or helped with the food or dealt with the dogs or got the table ready. Delicious food, good but light and easy conversation, no fuss or pretense. Such an undemanding but pleasant night was to form—the rambling farmhouse had always been homey and generous, from Tom's parents to Kelly and Tom taking it over. Zak folded into that with ease.

After dinner, Philip sat next to the fire, stealing glances and longer looks at Zak, who he could tell was stealing long looks and glances at him. He told himself to stop it and went right back to looking.

Tom was in the middle of retelling how he'd arrived and saved the day to get the enormous boulder moved exactly where Philip wanted. They'd each told their version and gone over moves and decisions like some kind of postmortem.

"…and then I yelled for Philip to pivot and Zak's amazing reach let him grab the bottom edge of the rock, but those quick feet kept him out of the way when it finally broke the right direction, and I just pushed and that's when it fell into place," Tom finished his fifth iteration of the events. He raised an arm and flexed. "My tackling prowess? Still got it."

"Dearest, how about taking that prowess into the kitchen and getting the brownies." Kelly pouted prettily. "I can barely stand to go another moment without one."

Tom set his beer down, kissed her forehead, and then looked at Philip. "Should I grab the cheesecake bites too?"

"Duh, cheesecake bites too."

"I'd hope so, given you suggested them as your fave and that's the whole reason I got them," Zak added.

Philip ignored Tom's laugh and let his eyes drift mostly shut. He didn't examine too closely how his comfort and ease at the house with Tom and Kelly wasn't affected by Zak's intrusion.

No. Intrusion was too harsh. But presence wasn't enough.

"When's the baby due?" Zak asked.

"Too long because I'm ready now. I feel like there's no bigger I can get." Kelly rested her hands on her belly and smiled. "What do you think, boy or girl? We made sure not to know."

Zak considered it a moment. "Definitely a girl."

"That's what we think too!" Kelly gestured at Philip and then herself. "Tom isn't set on a boy but he says he gets boy vibes. He's wrong, of course."

"Three against one—the odds aren't in his favor." Zak smiled. "Boy or girl, though, it doesn't matter. All babies are great."

"Yes they are. And mine is going to be the greatest." She studied Zak. "Do you have a kid? Know a kid? Or is this just a vague declaration about the goodness of babies?"

"None yet, and I'm the oldest of five by several years." Zak shrugged. "Mom and Dad had me young, got married while still pregnant and finished school, and then started on the rest of their lives and kids. Three brothers and one tiny sister, so I got a lot of baby years thanks to that."

"That sounds so wonderful."

"It was an absolute pain and each one of them are a menace, but I wouldn't change a thing," Zak said fondly.

Kelly squirmed to the escape her chair as she asked, "Want to see the nursery?"

"What? You know I do." Zak cupped her arm and steadied her stand and kept hold as they went through the house and disappeared upstairs.

Tom returned with the desserts piled on a platter and frowned. "I thought she couldn't live another moment without a brownie?"

"Brownies didn't stand a chance next to someone willing and eager to get the full nursery tour." Philip made a gimme motion and snagged several cheesecake bites before Tom could put the platter on the coffee table.

"Happy week-iversary. How's it going?"

"Easy, fine, nothing remarkable."

"What a careful answer." Tom smirked. "Better than expected, then."

Philip didn't rise to the bait. "It has been, actually. Zak isn't loud, doesn't seem to expect we'll be best buds, isn't around too much but when he is we get along, and he buys a ton of the good stuff groceries and doesn't label it all as his."

"Sounds like the perfect gentleman."

"A decent housemate."

Tom nodded slowly and hummed.

"What?"

"What, what?"

"I feel like you're trying to read into what isn't there." Philip polished off his cheesecake and thought about getting more.

Tom's slow nod turned into a speculative look.

"Okay really, what."

"You don't disclaim or caveat what you don't care about and never have. But you're saying a whole lot while trying to say as little as possible." Tom poked his own chest. "To me. The most practiced interpreter of you in all the land."

Philip did get more cheesecake, and then he shifted far back in the deep sofa. He could trust talking to Tom about finding Zak attractive and distracting and a disconcertingly right fit in his home. Tom would be gleeful but understanding and in the end try and get him reasoned through things. But the attraction was new and different—not like wanting to bang a random guy or talking each other out of stupidly banging the wrong person—and he wasn't ready to reveal that.

Only a week and it could be several, a lifetime, and barely a blip when he had five-some months yet to go. If he was honest about it, the awareness of Zak and it being different made him vulnerable and on very uncertain ground. He didn't want Tom to pry into that either.

So he went with "I might be almost bankrupt but my dick still works. I mean, I have a pulse, he's hot, and I noticed. Nothing more. You know how it is."

"I've had my share of those." Tom chuckled. "You've got almost six months left. Think you'll manage?"

"I can manage anything that's temporary." Movement caught Philip's eye and he watched Zak help Kelly down the stairs. Their gazes locked and Zak smiled. "Six months is nothing."

"Oh! Brownies," Kelly said and hustled across the room. She shamelessly loaded a plate and eased into the only chair she said she found comfortable and thus had been off-limits to anyone else for months. "Zak loves the nursery. Don't you?"

"I do, it's wonderful." Zak sat on the couch just-too-close to Philip and spread comfortably once settled, left knee almost touching Philip's thigh and his long arm resting on the back almost behind Philip.

The heat from Zak's hand and knee and person soaked into him immediately across the space separating them, and he could imagine what it'd feel like for Zak to stroke his nape. The thought-sensation made him roll his shoulder so he didn't otherwise react. Tom lifted an eyebrow at him so he shot back an *oh shut up* look.

"Kelly said you and Tom painted it. Twice, but without complaint, because she kept changing her mind. And built all the furniture," Zak said after he'd settled further into the couch and closer to Philip.

"Most of it from a kit, so don't be too impressed." Tom dutifully piled more brownies on Kelly's outstretched plate.

Zak nodded. "A fanciful barnyard is a clever theme—that's a nursery that could last a couple kids and then be a playroom when they're older."

Kelly pointed a brownie at Zak. "I like how you think, because that's what I was thinking."

"We're so clever. And all the animals are adorable."

"Adorable was the mission. We decided it'd be a bit strange to have realistic goats staring, unblinking, at the baby." Kelly widened her eyes comically and held two fingers up over them. "I adore our goats but those vertical pupils are unsettling."

"We can't take credit beyond the idea either—a local artist painted them." Tom leaned down to pat one of the dogs lolling nearby on the floor. "I championed including these guys, though. And Philip suggested the flock of birds in the trees and flying across the ceiling."

"That part was you?" Zak nudged Philip's shoulder.

"Yes. But adding birds to an outdoor scene isn't exactly vanguard."

"Maybe not but it was a good idea. I like the birds the best." Zak didn't take his hand away. "That's all the friends who'll visit the pollinator gardens, isn't it."

Philip smiled because Zak sounded so pleased about that.

Tom and Zak talked some football: college teams and players, the upcoming pro season. Both were interested and clearly glad to have company in that but not rabid. Philip tuned it out but liked the sound of their voices.

Zak said something that made him and Tom laugh. Their tone and conversation slipped him into that place when nostalgia fades to make you think about what's changed.

"There's got to be football things to do that's more than watching games. Right?" Philip said after their laughter and reminiscing quieted. "I mean, if you're missing it."

Zak considered him. "I haven't played or wanted to in years. That made me figure I'd moved on, but maybe I do miss it. Some aspects at least."

Philip shrugged. "Just a thought."

"A good one."

They subsided into mellow silence. Philip leaned forward to get more cheesecake and some brownies and when he sat back he let it be nearer still to Zak, right leg casually drawn up so their knees pressed together. He set the plate between them, no big deal, and Zak made a little noise and ate several of each. Philip reached for the last cheesecake bite and watched Zak's purposeful freeze mid-reach so they didn't touch hands.

Kelly sighed as she relaxed and started to doze. Tom caught the plate before it fell from her chair and started some football talk with Zak.

Zak answered and Philip didn't really listen. He concentrated on the throb of Zak's thigh pushed even harder to his knee and the feathery near-movement of Zak's finger on his neck. Zak's foot bounced and then stopped. He drummed his fingers on Philip's shoulder and then pulled away. He straightened, then slumped, and then crossed his ankles.

Philip hadn't noticed Zak as fidgety or impatient. "Everything okay?" he turned in to ask quietly.

"Everything's great I was just thinking… I'd like to get home soon. But whenever you're ready."

"I'm ready now," Philip surprised himself by saying.

Zak nodded, grabbed the plate, and stood up quick enough it almost unseated him.

"I'm about to join Kelly in falling asleep sitting here. Time for us to get going." Zak gathered napkins and bottles and carried them to the kitchen. He kept talking as he started to load the dishwasher. "Thanks for dinner and having me over and being on the rock-conquering team. Everything was super."

"Hey, our pleasure." Tom stood too and eyed Philip. "Sure you don't want to stay? There's no rush."

More than a few long dinners at the farm had Philip waking up on the couch to coffee and muffins. Tonight, cozy as the mood was, he didn't even consider that. "Say good night or good morning to Kelly for me." He gave the dogs quick ear scratchies and grabbed what Zak hadn't.

Tom followed them into the kitchen. "Leave the rest, there's not a lot anyway."

Zak spread cutlery he held in the basket and then lightly kicked the dishwasher door closed with his heel. He rinsed his hands and threw a wadded tea towel at Tom, which Tom caught and then tucked to his chest to run across the kitchen to the front door as if dodging tacklers.

They shared an up-top high five and a bro hug. Philip shook his head at them but didn't mind Tom's arm thrown across his shoulders on the short walk to the truck.

"Drive safe—the deer are gonna be out and way distracted." Tom opened the passenger door for Philip and then retreated to the porch.

"Yes, boss," Zak said.

Philip watched the moon and Zak drove slowly enough to brake for three deer and one scurrying possum. The house shone a beacon through the trees and for a moment Philip thought about where he'd go if he lost it. He hadn't come up with an answer before Zak parked, and they got out of the truck and to the front door.

Zak didn't go in. Tension radiated from Zak but Philip stayed loose. He wasn't certain of the cause and didn't want to snarl things up with guessing. Zak still didn't go in and for a while didn't say anything more, so Philip stood waiting. The night air was cool but not cold, and the forest noises had started to thaw into full spring.

"Moon's good tonight." Zak huffed a laugh. He sounded nervous.

"She always is—but then I say that every time I see her."

"Me too." Zak squared to face Philip. "I need to ask you something."

"Hopefully I have the answer."

"Let me say upfront that I'm mortified if I'm wrong, and I'm sorry? If I have the wrong idea or it's the kind of thing to apologize for. But also that it's okay if I'm wrong, we'll consider it a blip and keep it moving." Zak took tentative hold of Philip's upper arm. "I don't think I am, though."

Philip wasn't sure how to answer that. Not a question, and not really clear what Zak meant. He tingled all over—anticipation and knowing even as part of him denied it—and Zak's grip on his arm tightened. Zak's other hand skated up his neck and cupped Philip's cheek. Philip lifted his face. He'd been right, he'd known all along, that Zak wanted to kiss him. Would kiss him.

Zak's kiss was gentle but firm. He opened against Philip's lips and tilted, softly licked the corner of Philip's mouth, and tilted again. Then Zak sighed and rested his forehead to Philip's and his hold became an embrace.

"That was okay?" Zak eventually whispered.

Philip answered by kissing Zak, pressing his hands into the small of Zak's back and them together. Zak accepted the kiss, and nothing deeper, and then moved a step back. The wind picked up, pushing clouds along, and the moon reappeared.

"There she is." Zak glanced toward the sky and then stared at Philip, eyes dark in the silvery light and serious. "Maybe it's unnecessary but I have to be certain. That *was* okay? And I didn't totally just freak you out?"

"More than okay." Zak made no further sign of interest, so Philip let his hands fall away.

"I wasn't sure about me as much as you," Zak confessed. "It's probably painfully obvious I've never kissed a guy before—never wanted to. Or had to try and figure out if they'd want to be kissed. But since meeting you, I've wanted to."

"And now you have." Philip was tempted to add something flip and even unkind, but he bit that back. He wasn't sure what Zak wanted and Zak wasn't giving him any clues. He hoped if that was it, and already done, they really could consider it a blip as Zak said.

Then they stayed like that—close, not touching, sort of avoiding one another's gaze—for too long.

Philip sighed. "Look, I'm definitely not freaking out so don't you go freaking out."

"I won't. That much I'm confident about." Zak's expression turned speculative. "Are you not freaking out because you're super chill or do you want guys to kiss you?"

"You didn't read me wrong. We're good."

"That's something… that's good. Is it ridiculous to say thank you?"

"No."

Zak waited but didn't say more and Philip didn't offer anything else, so he nodded and went to the door. Philip followed and tried to make sense of what all happened, there. His whole body buzzed, mind noisy and his hands oddly numb, not from excitement or even a quickened pulse but with disappointment.

By tacit agreement they left the light off. It seemed easier somehow to be in the foyer together without having to see. He was half out of his coat and toeing at his shoes when he wobbled and grabbed Zak's arm so he didn't fall over. The contact jolted through him. Zak grabbed his shoulders and crowded him against the closed front door.

"Did you want *me* to kiss you?"

"Yes." Philip's voice quavered.

Zak yanked Philip's coat to the ground and his barely controlled noise of want cut through Philip's middle. He crushed Philip to him, lifted, and staggered toward the stairs. His next kiss was hard and probing and forced Philip to open, wide and wider, begged Philip to respond.

Philip had no hesitation. He clawed the back of Zak's sweater and shirt into a bunch and pulled as Zak climbed the two landing stairs. Zak pushed Philip to the wall, raised his arms, and undulated as Philip stripped them away, and growled back into their kiss. They tripped and scrabbled upstairs, rattled the walls.

At the top Zak shifted them around enough to get his hands in Philip's shirt, got trapped in the flannel and, not feeling skin, uttered a low curse and ripped it off. The cuffs stuck at Philip's wrists so he ripped those open too.

Philip pulled and twisted until the hem of his shirt untucked and Zak's hands gave chase. Zak groaned into his mouth and caressed him, scattershot, as if wanting to touch everywhere at once, before wrapping him in close.

He bucked against Zak's thigh in sharp, uncontained movements, and then he lifted his thigh to the heat and readiness of Zak's cock.

Zak's breath caught and he said something guttural and indistinct, but Philip understood. He dug into Zak's belt loops and tugged them into his room.

Philip kept hold when Zak shoved him down on the bed and used the leverage to open Zak's button and fly, and before Zak could crawl over him, he turned his wrists so he could press his palms to the sleek of Zak's hips. Then he stilled.

Not turning on the lights meant his eyes were already adjusted and he moved his hands an increment inward and watched Zak's labored breath, the taut heave of abdomen and chest, Zak's expression. Almost a grimace, then Zak's mouth went lax and wanting, and then Zak tightened his jaw and decided.

Strong fingers captured Philip's wrists and Zak pulled one up to kiss the pulse point. His lips lingered as his other hand found, lightly touched, and then started stroking Philip's cock.

Philip's legs curled inward and his solar plexus contracted at the touch, at the neediness Zak willingly showed. He tightened his hand into a fist and squeezed, let up, squeezed again. He stroked Zak in quick motions and then slowed to drag from base to tip, and then he loosened his grip and left his thumb over Zak's slit.

The contact was so hot there, boldly intimate, barely leashed.

Zak fucked into his fist several times, mindless in motion and rhythm. Then he stuttered to a halt and opened his eyes to look down at Philip's hold and then into Philip's eyes. Zak's crooked grin flashed and he slid to the floor to stand, peeled Philip's pants and briefs and socks away, and then he pushed until Philip elbow-walked to lie righted on the bed.

Philip could have come just from Zak's heat and size pinning him to the mattress, from the insistent prod of Zak's cock aligning with his, from the unforgiving clamp of Zak's arm reaching beneath him to get their hips even closer together.

This was what he had wanted. What he'd craved.

He let out a long breath and made himself wait. He needed to feel the heat and size and weight a bit longer. Zak sensed this and waited too, and with each exhale rocked ever-so, as if to remind Philip of their position and the pressure and Zak's complete hold of him.

Philip wrapped his hands around Zak's shoulders and reveled in the tension, the sheen of sweat, the trembling that deepened the longer Zak remained. A moment, a moment longer, and then suddenly it was too much and not nearly enough. He tilted his head back and shoved his hands down to dig into Zak's ass, and Zak waited no longer.

It could only be fast, now. They rutted so hard the floor protested and the bed shifted away from the wall. Philip raised his legs and gripped Zak's ribs, his toes curling at the rise of Zak's hips.

Zak fucked against him again and again, and then pried from their messy kiss to lift onto his hands, palms flattened to the mattress. He watched as he made Philip come—made Philip watch him come—and then slowly he stopped moving until all they did was gaze at each other and fight to breathe.

Overstimulation finally made Philip break. Every nerve vibrated, sensitized and attuned and answering the burn of Zak's body and touch. His dick throbbed and tried to stir, and his hips rolled in escape and pursuit. When he shifted, Zak moved too but didn't let him get far. He muttered as Zak tugged him into a kiss, moved so heavy yet restive as Zak caressed him everywhere, and then oblivion claimed him.

Zak woke him to demand he come again, held tight in the curve and heat of Zak's body and fist, Zak wet and hard between his thighs.

He woke to Zak's slow kisses and persuasive hands and could only sigh encouragement and slurred breath as they lazily ground against each other in a dreamy haze.

When next he woke, the sun neared midday, bright, and he was alone.

He grunted and rolled to flip his old-school alarm clock upright. Almost eleven. Philip dropped it on the table and scraped the crust from his eyes and then let his arms fold across his face. The room kinda stunk—he stunk and his skin itched—and that wasn't something he usually minded in a morning after, but it bothered him now, lying there in the empty bed and terrible quiet.

Had Zak gone for a run? Gone to town? Fled the scene and gone entirely? Philip cursed it and hated that he cared. At least laundry and a shower and sewing the buttons back on his shirt would occupy his day. But he was pissed the languid enjoyment of hella good afterglow and lounging in achy satisfaction was ruined.

If he discovered Zak had left, ruined was more like angry and disappointed and more that he wouldn't admit.

"Psst, are you awake?" Zak whispered and lightly tapped the wall.

Philip's heart jumped into his throat and he almost shot out of bed. He might have drifted back to sleep but he couldn't tell. Years of feigning sleep in worse settings let him continue to lie there breathing deep and easy.

Zak padded to the bed and Philip sensed him staring, gauging, maybe seeing the slight tremble in his hands. He stayed standing there and Philip kept hiding through the count of ten, and then twenty, and then Philip lost count.

Annoyance and curiosity won out and Philip moved an arm and cracked open an eye to get a look at Zak.

"Morning." Zak drummed his thighs and Philip worked not to be distracted by him in only his jeans, and was helped some when Zak lowered to kneel beside the bed. He flattened his hands on the mattress and set his shoulders. "Before anything else—last night." Zak's gray eyes were earnest.

Philip had no reason to be disappointed about this or surprised. But he should probably invent a reason to hit the road for the remainder of their five months and almost three weeks deal. He straightened and shifted to lean on the headboard because it distanced him from Zak. It also pulled the covers low to his hips and he watched Zak notice, zone out and flush with color, and then refocus. He tugged the blankets higher but Zak reached over and traced a knuckle across his abdomen, stilling the action.

"This didn't go at all as I intended." Zak smiled and rested his chin on his other hand.

"No?" he asked dryly.

Zak drew lazy lines following the almost-revealing hang of the sheet aproning Philip's lap, and Philip tried not to react. But he couldn't keep from moving entirely, and when he shifted in an abrupt jerk, Zak smiled and then blinked. Zak sighed, squeezed Philip's arm, and seemed to hesitate before letting go.

"I'm already ahead of myself again. Just a sec." Zak rose from his crouch and went into the hall and then returned with a tray.

Oatmeal with all of Zak's favorite trimmings, coffee exactly as Philip liked it, and half a banana. Nothing fancy or different but it made him wary. It seemed conciliatory. It made stupid tears prick his eyes.

"I'd have breakfast with you but I sort of was starving and wolfed mine down as your coffee brewed."

Philip sipped the coffee and then despite it being scalding, thirst demanded he nearly gulp it down. Zak held out a hand and after a moment Philip gave him the empty mug. He drained the water Zak got from the bathroom tap and shook his head when Zak offered to get more. Then he made inroads on the oatmeal, too hungry to refuse it and the barrier it provided.

Zak sat on the edge of the bed and kept his hands fisted in his lap. "There's no great way to explain this."

"Then just say it. It's fine."

"Wise words." Zak met his gaze. "I had this whole slow play planned—you wouldn't believe how suave and subtle yet determined and irresistible I was going to be. And, well…." He actually blushed. "I'm not sorry for jumping your bones, but I am sorry I went from thinking you're attractive to jumping your bones without even treating you to a little of my seduction campaign first."

Warmth charged Philip's spine, filling his head and lungs and groin. It was dizzying, slammed him from cold retreat into possibility. Of what he wasn't sure but he wanted it—even last night he hadn't admitted how much he wanted Zak and six months of whatever this would be—and he allowed the want.

He must have sat too long trying to catch his breath because Zak nodded and turned from him.

"To be clear, I can deal with a one-night stand situation too. I get it, they happen, last night was amazing but it can stay as an only last night thing. I promise I won't be an asshole or get vindictive about our agreement."

"We could change our agreement."

Zak turned bodily to look at Philip. "What?" He frowned. "That is a fair point, and true. I don't have to stay, even."

"No, I mean…." Philip slid sideways so he could press two fingers to Zak's lips and then drag them down to the pulse point at the base of Zak's throat. "What all were you planning to do to me?"

Zak made a low sound and swallowed. "You know, sitting with you like this I can't really remember. Or think." He closed his eyes as if to concentrate. "Definitely create more opportunities to undress in front of you, dinner in town, long walks, always coming home with bear claws, finding you excellent rocks and logs and wildflowers to seed. My big move was to find enormous hunks of slate and lay them as a path to the overlook."

"Yard work as seduction?"

"Would it have worked?"

"It could be added to my terms. Especially rocks as gifts." Philip savored the surge of Zak's heartbeat against his touch, and then he had to smile. "And obviously—obviously it'd work."

"We can still go to dinner." Zak's eyes danced. His whole body relaxed and then readied like a spring.

"I'd rather eat in." Philip furrowed his hand down past the button of Zak's jeans.

"I was going to talk you into showering with me after breakfast, but that can't happen."

"No?"

"Not yet anyway." Zak half stood, popped his jeans undone—hard and ready and intent—and stepped from them as he grabbed Philip's leg.

Philip twisted to set the tray in an almost controlled crash land on the floor as he was pulled, urgently, to the center of the bed and under Zak. His hips juddered at first touch and Zak laughed, rumbly and pleased, and they grappled the sheet away and met for a kiss.

Chapter Five

THEY NEVER made it out of bed or to the shower. Philip woke the next morning satisfied and complacent, and once more alone, but more in desperate need of a shower than breakfast on a tray. He scrubbed everywhere twice and slathered on the good-smelling lotion. Then he got dressed in something comfy and stripped the bed.

He got downstairs to Zak dressed in nicer clothes and looking ready to go.

"Good morning. I was about to wake you up but wanted to let you sleep until the last minute." Zak propped a foot on the bench in the foyer and tied his dress shoes. "I have to be in the city by tonight and stay a few days. There's a quarterly meeting I can't skip, and don't want to because there's some major decisions on the line for my giving projects."

"Giving projects?"

"Grants, philanthropy, environmental causes, playfields and centers in underserved communities. I have all this money, so I hired people to find good ways for me to spend it beyond investments."

"That's commendable."

"And some would say for the tax breaks." Zak shrugged and then looked at Philip. "I should have woken you an hour ago so this wasn't cut and run. Sorry."

"It's no big deal."

Zak kissed Philip's cheek and then closed his eyes and hurried out the door. "Like I said, only a few days."

Philip followed to stand on the flagstones. "Hope your meetings go well. And you find a lot of worthy causes to fund."

"Thanks. See you soon." Zak put on a pair of sunglasses, got into and revved his truck, and then was gone.

Philip stood there and shifted his hold on their wad of filthy sheets and tried not to feel cheap. Not quite a freak-out, but not quite reassuring to Philip's niggling suspicion Zak and his night was destined to be a one and done.

He went inside and grumped at the thoughtfulness of coffee percolating and started the wash. Philip had plenty to do and catch up with, and should be glad to get time alone and days left to his own devices.

Instead he didn't exactly mope around but he didn't get much accomplished. He kept thinking of things to tell Zak or wished he had help in the yard and very much noticed the difference of lying in an empty bed.

Midmorning of the fifth day, he pretended to weed and transplant from his woodsy nursery into the pollinator beds, but was too antsy to be productive. He stood holding the shovel, gazing into the trees more than anything.

When he heard an approaching engine and the crunch of tires, his pulse spiked. Heat flushed his skin and tightened his middle.

"Get a grip," he whispered, and then after a beat, he sped to the corner of the house, spied Zak's truck, and before Zak could catch him looking, hurried back to the garden. He made busy with some weeds and didn't react to the sound of Zak's footsteps on the patio.

"I thought I'd find you out here."

Philip waited, waited a bit longer, and then straightened. Zak was dressed casually, hair wind-tossed, hands loose at his sides but the rest of him coiled.

"Welcome back," Philip said evenly, prepared for Zak's curiosity and horniness to be sated and for them to pleasantly ignore what happened.

Zak strode into the garden and bore in, kicked the shovel away and hauled Philip into his arms, hands finding Philip's shoulders, then hips, then ass, mouth finding Philip's neck and earlobe and lips.

"That was a damn long four days," Zak said with a faint pant when he finally broke their kiss. "I wanted to do that before I left but then I'd never have gone."

The crimp at Philip's heart eased and he massaged his hands up Zak's shoulders. "Did good projects get approved?"

"Many, I'm happy to report."

"Tell me about them," Philip asked and would be glad to listen.

"Later," Zak said distractedly. His eyes were dark and heavy and hot, and his gaze crisscrossed Philip's face and collarbones and bare arms. He pressed their hips together. "In the middle of anything important?"

"Not really."

"Wanna go to bed?"

Philip couldn't resist that. "Lead the way."

They spent the rest of that day in bed too.

The following morning they had breakfast as Philip preferred, in the kitchen, and every morning after. Stealing bites of fruit from each other's hand, oatmeal cooking and maybe scalding as they necked and groped and pretended to make plans for the afternoon. Sometimes yard work, sometimes a hike in the forestland, sometimes making out on the couch.

Zak got up far too early most days, leaving Philip to grumble in bed and fall back to sleep, waiting to be roused with kisses and a quick come and long shower after.

Once Zak asked if it'd be all right to invite colleagues to the house and Philip had said of course. Once he'd suggested they go on a weekend road trip somewhere. After the initial mention they hadn't discussed either again.

Next mornings blurred one into another, and Philip lost track of days and abandoned even the pretense of writing or finding a gig as a week and then more slid by. There was plenty he could worry about but all he wanted for the moment was this, and the worries would still be there when Zak really had gone.

Philip had his camera out to get before and after pics of the backyard, and then he started bringing it and a long lens on their hikes. It'd been forever since he'd wanted to take pictures. Being on assignment was nothing like existing and observing and capturing what followed his whim. His shots of birds and landscapes and crumbling fieldstone walls were unremarkable, but doing the work felt good. Showing them to Zak, always so eager to see—even better.

Photos with Zak, or simply of Zak, dominated pictures of rocks and mountains, and he was less sure what to do with those. He kept them tucked away in a file; something else he could deal with later. Zak gave no indication of worry or freak-out, future or otherwise. It permitted them to ignore everything except in the moment only and Philip accepted that.

"What are you thinking about?"

"A few things." Philip had perched on the bar counter to eat and was finishing his coffee while Zak tidied.

They were comfortable in sweats and tees and the day promised to be sunny and mild, but Philip had no motivation beyond napping in its warmth. Zak hadn't gone anywhere that morning, so they'd woken together, slowly, several times. Which suited Philip fine.

"Vague, but nothing bad, so I'll intuit it's about me." Zak dried his hands and tossed the towel aside. "It is me, right?"

He looked Zak up and down. "Parts of you."

"Which parts?" He licked his lips as he crossed the room and then split Philip's legs wider to crowd in between them.

"Like I'm just gonna tell you?"

"Well, what if I want to hear it? And if I ask super nicely?"

"You'll never get it out of me." Philip smiled against Zak's throat.

Zak boosted onto his toes and wrapped an arm around Philip's waist so he could slot their hips together. "Challenge accepted." He caught Philip's hand and kissed Philip's palm. "That part?"

"Nope." Philip leaned back and let Zak take his weight. He yelped when Zak nipped a finger, and shook his head. "Not those parts, either."

"Hmmm, maybe these?" Zak asked as he moved Philip's hand from shoulder to shoulder and then to his sternum.

"Nah."

Zak put Philip's hand on his thigh and raised an eyebrow. Philip yawned and mouthed *no*. Zak tried his ear, his knee, raised his shirt to skate Philip's knuckles under his belly button.

"No, none of that." Philip's legs tensed in a little jump when Zak moved his hand lower, fingertips slipping past rumpled sweats to coarse hair and hot skin, but he kept his expression blank.

"I think I'm getting warmer." Zak rolled his hips and grinned when Philip groaned. "Definitely warmer." He opened his hand to fully cradle Philip's and then covered his cock with their hold. "This part?"

He waited and Zak waited him out, smiling while rocking against his palm but nothing more. Philip heaved a breath and turned his hips, tucked his heels under Zak's butt, and shoved his pants down with his free hand.

"You got me," he breathed.

Zak laughed. "Damn right I do."

Hollow, sharp metal thumped and voices sounded. Noise from the road never reached the house. Philip started to pull from Zak, and then he tried to slither backward when someone knocked on the front door, but Zak held him steady.

The knock sounded again and Zak shook with effort and then called, "Yeah?"

Philip gave Zak an incredulous look.

"Coach?" a voice asked from the direction of the front door.

Zak's hand tightened and Philip smothered a moan in his neck.

"Braden? Be right there—you boys meet me out back."

A slight pause, murmured voices, and then apparently Braden answered an affirmative and the door closed.

"Fuuuuuuck," Zak huffed and lowered his head onto Philip's. "They're early. That and I totally forgot about them."

"Who?" Philip asked even as Zak was moving to haul him nearer and stroke them, held together in one broad hand, hard and fast.

He wanted to protest. He wanted Zak to stroke them raw. He heard Braden and who knew who else, their car doors and discussion and footsteps way too close.

"It's bright outside and dark in here… I can't—I can't stop, and I can't go out there like this." Zak's voice was strained and ragged.

Philip's eyes fluttered closed when Zak squeezed them just right and without thinking, he stilled to make the sensation and the suspension before completion last.

"No you don't—we're almost there. You are. I can feel it," Zak panted. He moved to prod the delicate span of flesh behind Philip's balls with his thumb, pushing more and then more. "Please, c'mon, come for me."

Philip did come, more from Zak's words than touch. Zak jerked against him and then hauled him into a kiss.

They kissed for too long until Zak wrenched away with a frustrated noise. He undressed, scrubbed down in the sink, dug in the laundry and then hopped around getting into some work clothes.

"Sorry about that… but not sorry." Zak wetted a fresh towel and left it beside Philip after pausing for a brief kiss. "Meet me on the patio when you can." He sped from the kitchen and instead of just leaving by the sliding glass door, went to the front and around.

Philip slid bonelessly into a half lean on the counter, shifted so he could let his head drop onto it, and sucked wind. A chorus of cheers went up and then Zak's voice rose, words indistinct, and Philip hooked his elbow on the counter and steadied on his feet. He ignored the damp towel in favor of a shower—lukewarm to kick the heaviness enveloping him—and found some clothes.

"All right, explain," he said as he approached Zak.

His backyard swarmed with teenagers, busy and talking and paying them no mind.

"Big pavers to win you over, remember?"

"What gave you the impression that's still necessary?" Philip looked meaningfully toward the house and then dragged his gaze up Zak's whole body, slowing at Zak's middle with a knowing smile. "Unless you want to prove your interest, again."

Zak snagged Philip's waistband and tugged them closer and let his hand flirt up under Philip's shirt.

Ghost sensations from the kitchen skittered across Philip's skin and through his core. It required effort to offer Zak the tall thermos of water he'd brought out.

Zak smiled and rubbed small circles at the small of Philip's back.

"Water?" Philip cleared his throat and then repeated the question without sounding choked.

It shouldn't be that Zak could get him hot and bothered and ready so soon after making him come in the kitchen—and without more than light contact and an appreciative look—sort of hidden from a pack of teenage boys no less. But there he stood, dick twitching and his pulse rising as he contemplated how to discreetly drag Zak inside.

"Hey, thanks. I was just about to complain that something made me damn thirsty." Zak winked and then drank the thermos empty in enormous gulps.

Philip watched Zak's throat work and listened to the gasp of breath after with far too much attunement and sighed. He wanted to lift the water droplets at the corner of Zak's mouth away with his thumb, but instead marched to the kitchen, refilled the thermos, and returned bearing coffee and a selection of fruit.

"Okay, once again—explain."

"Very nice," Zak said and took his preferred mug and an apple. "Instead of our usual training and drills, I'm having the boys help me with this, as a little change of pace. That and I can use the help."

"And who are the boys, exactly?"

"The defense squad." At Philip's blank expression, Zak perked an eyebrow. "From the high school football team."

"Why is the high school football team at my house and how did you come to invite them?"

"Just the defense." Zak ate nearly half the apple in one bite. He swiped his lips and pointed around the yard. "Braden and the big four with him are seniors, the rest are on down. The high school is small so there's no varsity or JV team. Braden's dad hooked me up with the slate—freebies from an old quarry on their property."

"I like freebies, and I like slate. I still don't know why or how any of this is relevant to them being here, doing this for you."

Zak frowned. "Did I never tell you? I swore I had." He finished the apple and tossed the core into the trees, wiped his hand on his pants, and then cupped Philp's nape. "You never hear 'I'm back from practice' in the mornings, do you."

That stirred a vague recognition in Philip but not enough to make anything click. "And you should be aware there's only a few things I'm capable of focusing on when first awake."

High color stained Zak's cheeks at the inference. "I should have mentioned it again over dinner or something. But it honestly felt so comfortable and routine so quickly I kinda forgot you didn't fully know."

Philip scanned the yard. "I sure do now."

"Really, these boys are here doing this because of you."

"Me. Because they're laying pavers?"

"No, not that part. I gave a lot of thought to what you said about my missing football and suggesting I find a way to reconnect with it. Only a few days later in town, Braden and his pals started talking to me—I guess word is out I'm living here—and asked if I could show them a few things."

"You're that notable, are you?" Philip teased. "I'm impressed."

"Only in certain circles. What's a good analogy—hmm, say, a reporter of some renown who already has a prestigious award under his belt."

Philip conceded the point with a nod.

Zak grinned. "Anyway, I decided one better than showing them a few things and done. I've been punishing them with morning conditioning and drills at the high school field ever since."

"That's not because of me."

"It is. And it was a good insight." Zak caressed Philip's neck and then gave him a gentle shake. "I figured out I didn't miss football so much as the camaraderie and working toward a goal, that kind of stuff. I wouldn't have parsed all that and found the missing parts of football again, started coaching these dorks otherwise to then have at my beck and call and pretend it's a workout."

Silly, fond warmth filled Philip's chest that Zak had listened, and that it'd made Zak happy. "Better than us and Tom throwing out our backs doing it."

"See? Exactly. And speaking of, I want to get Tom in and run some drills and get them a solid start on the season. He knows his stuff and he'd do great with the guys, but I figured it'd be good to wait until after the baby. Don't you think?"

Such a comfortable, normal, part of his life conversation. Philip did quick mental math and wondered if Zak realized their six months would be over with the baby still new and football not yet started. He should remind them of it, push a boundary or two back into place.

Instead he said, "Tom would enjoy that. And waiting for everything-baby to settle makes sense."

Zak nodded. "Cool. And I hope all this today is cool too. You did say it was all right if I invited some colleagues over."

"I did and it is fine, but let's say it's not quite what I expected based on that."

"I only talk to tech dweebs in black turtlenecks and puffy vests via video call—not just anyone gets to come here." Zak glanced around, kissed behind Philip's ear, once softly and again with force and promise, and then pulled fully away. "I don't mind if they see but if they do, this'll turn into razzing me for ages, and I want this done, not them distracted."

Philip paused a beat. "Do they know that you and I are"—he gestured vaguely—"whatever we are?"

"Nope. Honestly, at first I wasn't ready to share that with anyone else. It's not exactly early morning coach talk anyway or really their business." Zak nudged bodily into Philip. "But me not minding is separate from recognizing you get a say in that too."

Despite there being no change in Zak's easy demeanor, Philip could tell his answer mattered. He respected Zak's reasoning and didn't want to be a jerk but could also use this to reassert that their situation was temporary.

"And that's much appreciated." Philip watched Zak's eyes focus go from his hands to his mouth to his eyes. His awareness flashed to being in the kitchen a bit ago, and thoughts of pointing anything out burned away, unimportant. "It's pretty much how I'd approach it. I don't need anyone to know but if they find out, they do. And if the team does, well, I'll deal. Just…." Philip raised a finger. "No tongue."

"No tongue, got it." Zak grinned and handed Philip his empty mug to start walking backward. "Remember, this is part of your wooing, so dig in with the rest of us or kick back on the patio—your choice."

Philip rolled his eyes, but Zak caught his smile right before turning around. He sat to finish his coffee in slow sips and ate an orange, watching Zak guide and boss and interact with the team.

Zak was good with them, and they clearly thought Zak hung the moon.

"Relatable," Philip muttered and got to his feet. *Foolish*, he thought next.

He'd planned to lounge and observe but he liked yard work and wanted to be out there with Zak doing it. So he got his gloves and joined the knot of them making their way to the overlook, tearing a strip through the grass. Zak beamed at him over the handle of his grub hoe and he stuck out his tongue, but Zak stared at him long enough to catch his eventual smile.

The team had come armed with a variety of tools and hauling equipment and a load of sand. They muscled the pavers from Braden's truck into place with an ease Philip envied. Zak involved them in discussion of what pavers to use where, for fit and design and flow, and they all checked in with Philip for final approval.

He gave it, easily. After small tweaks and a show of grumbling this or that.

They made it to the overlook and Philip stepped out of the way, buried the shovel in the ground, and leaned on the handle. He'd leave breaking up the hardpack and getting the circle laid to them.

One of the kids peeled from the group and trotted over. Liam, he remembered—Liam with the twin brother, both hulking seniors who lived on a dairy farm and looked like they could each lift a cow.

"Looking good, isn't it?" Liam said as if they were old farmhands on a break.

"It's looking real good. You guys are doing fine work."

"Leif and me brought a ton of fieldstones. Coach said if we had time and hunks of narrow slate we'd do a rounded wall at the end here, kinda make it a bench." Liam gestured a big U-shape in the air and then checked his phone. "I think we have time!" he called over a shoulder and then looked at Philip. "That is if you want a wall."

"A wall sounds perfect."

"That's what I think too. It's Coach's idea. But Braden showed us how to tap the slate with hammers and split it, so having enough of that shouldn't be an issue."

Philip almost laughed at Liam's matter-of-fact appraisal of the situation. It was sweet and confident and straightforward, and he was certain some of that confidence came from working with Zak.

"I definitely want a try at shaping some slate."

"Me too! And if we mess any up it can just go in the path gaps." Liam nodded. "I'll let Coach know the wall is a go."

Philip didn't keep out of the way for the bench wall building. He did actually want to try his hand at splitting slate, and it took several of them to stack rocks just right and then hold the slate level to wedge gaps and fill in lifts. They used a bit of mortar to attach the top but otherwise let fit and gravity do the work of holding the wall together.

He trotted away when detail and then clean-up work began. Since this was a gift and all, he could let them do that.

"Don't go out front!" Zak called as he neared the house.

Philip waved, grabbed their mugs and his orange peel, and ducked inside. He ran upstairs, fired off a quick text to Tom, slammed down two glasses of water, got more for Zak, and then settled on the patio.

About a half hour later, the boys were almost out of steam and the whole job was nearly done. Braden, Liam, and Zak had disappeared, so Philip went to the overlook pad and supervised, mostly to tell everyone they'd done plenty and could call it a day.

His small, hard patch at the edge of the world had expanded into the gently oblong curving rock wall, large paved area, and room for chairs. He stepped over the bench and lowered onto it carefully and smiled. At the perfect height of the stones, a perfect view, the several vultures wheeling high above the river. After a moment he became aware of expectant silence and twisted around.

"Ta-da," Zak said and spread his arms.

A simple but beautiful metal and mesh fireplace sat in the center of everything.

"Braden, did your dad get this out back of your place too?" Philip asked. He got up and gave it a once-over, and found himself tracing the design cut into black metal, circles and crescents representing moon phases with the full moon. S'mores and blankets and coziness, he thought, and met Zak's waiting gaze. Zak nodded, knowing that he remembered, knowing that he found the moon and understood.

"Do you like it okay or can I have it? Coach said second dibs if you decided nah," one of the boys said.

The team shouted for him to decide and laughed, but before he answered, their attention was completely stolen by Tom's loud yell across the yard.

"Did someone order pizza?"

A general cheer went up followed by a near stampede of Tom. The team divvied the boxes stacked almost past the top of Tom's head and returned to the overlook to chow down.

Zak moved to stand beside Philip. "I've been thinking about how to feed this mob." He took hold of Philip's hand. "Thank you."

"No biggie. They've earned it."

"It can be no biggie and also be great." Zak jiggled their hands. "After this they'll like you more than me."

"Pizza is fleeting. Football hero worship is forever." Philip joined his fingertip with one of the crescent moons. "The fireplace is marvelous, but I'm thinking it wasn't a found freebie."

"No, it wasn't. But you do like it?"

"I was excited when the boys laid a fire ring with leftover fieldstones. This getting set inside that ring is next level." Philip tapped the metal. "I do like it, a lot. It's so well made it's like a sculpture—I can't wait to see a fire glowing in it."

"That's what I thought when I saw it. An art piece for the yard." Zak smiled and ran a finger along the patterns in the fireplace until they touched, and then moved to cover his hand.

Philip glanced at the team—busy eating and talking about the job they'd just finished. Tom, talking with them but casting an eye to him and Zak. Kelly, one hand shielding her eyes from the sun boring a hole in him standing there. He also didn't mind, but he also didn't want to give it away like this.

"Probably a good time to introduce the team to Tom?"

"Good call." Zak gave Philip's hand a squeeze, snapped his fingers, and then waded into the pizza melee.

Philip walked the new path to the patio to check on Kelly.

"Everything looks amazing! Even better than I imagined." She held a pizza box in one hand and two slices of pizza, crusts out, like a sandwich in the other.

"You knew to imagine this?"

"Sure. Zak texted me pictures of the slate he'd found like a week ago and wanted my opinion on it." She had a big bite of her pizza sandwich and made a happy noise. "But Tom told him where to get the outdoor fireplace."

"He's a true friend." Philip got Kelly eased into a chair and sat opposite her.

"He's been wanting one for the farm. After seeing yours in place, we'll definitely have it by next week." She dropped the pizza box on the table and opened it between them. "I ate a medium mushroom and eggplant for the drive over so I won't snarl if you have some. We got so many, though, pepperoni and cheeseburger and I don't know what else, so if you want more than plain cheese, it's out there."

"Cheese is great. And did I say Tom was the true friend?"

"We both are, so long as you don't ask how much you owe us for it."

"Emotional blackmail, wow."

Kelly waved an imperious hand. "Eat your dang pizza."

Philip followed her lead and had two slices at once. Plain, loaded, whatever, he didn't care. He was starved and had learned early to fill up on whatever came his way. Life hadn't allowed the luxury of choice most days.

"Zak's been so excited to do this. He's just incredibly adorable, right?" Kelly let a pause build but Philip didn't rise to her insinuations, so she shrugged and moved on. "It is really better than I imagined. And I think worth today's onslaught, but I hope the invasion of your space and sanctity hadn't been too rough."

"I haven't hated it."

"That's something." Kelly sounded pert and a touch disbelieving.

"I actually haven't. The kids are easy—I mean, Zak's riding herd, not me—and I sure couldn't get this done in a day, so that alone is worth the intrusion." Philip watched Zak, simply appreciating strength and fluid movement and then reined his thoughts back in. "It does look amazing."

"You know, after everything that led to this, I'd say you kinda lucked out."

"I kinda did." Philip leaned forward conspiratorially. "I'm glad he didn't wind up with all my furniture, though."

Kelly snickered and then made a thoughtful face. Philip braced for her to make another veiled hint or observe the furniture was, for all intents, basically Zak's too at the moment. At the very least shared.

"Do you have some lemonade? I could super go for some lemonade."

"I'll go check." He made a pitcher with the rest of their lemons and the perfect oversaturation of sugar, and then filled two glasses with ice.

"Exactly what I wanted, thank you." Kelly drank the glass down, drained a refill, and closed her eyes.

A minute later she began snoring softly, so he went to contemplate the new path, wanting to see everything again, appreciate the pavers and lush growth spring had brought to the backyard.

Philip discovered pavers were laid along the side of the house to join the patio as well as from the patio to the overlook. They'd also made a short fieldstone wall not quite knee-high, and hadn't wrecked any of his ferns and flowers to do it, carving out only enough room for them between the house and the woods, vibrant with blooming spring beauties and periwinkle. It made the once muddy pass-through into an enchanted portal.

"Mr. C?"

One of the not-seniors stood on the path at the corner of the house. Brown hair, brown eyes, in simple clothes and basic work boots. He seemed too lanky and thin for football, much less defense, but Philip understood the dynamics of small towns and taking what you can get. Philip also recognized a specific alertness in the kid, and a hunger that went far deeper than the teenage years of being a veritable garbage disposal.

"Grady?" he chanced.

"Yep." Grady smiled. "I just wanted to say thanks for having us all over today, and thanks for the pizza."

Philip gestured around them. "Pretty sure you did me the favor. Come back tomorrow—I've got some grapevine to chop out and trees that need clearing."

Grady hesitated. "I know you're kidding, but if you ever do need an extra pair of hands, I'd be glad for the work. Even for more pizza or something would be fine."

"I'll keep that in mind." Philip guided them to the patio.

The sun was long in late afternoon and the team were slowly cleaning up. Their lack of speed was obvious as not willing to let the good day end more than anything. They shouted at each other, admired their handiwork, carted tools and leavings back to their vehicles, lingered.

"Did you get enough to eat?" Philip made sure to sound casual as he and Grady watched the proceedings continue to wind down. "Tom showed up ready to feed an army, and I think there's a few apples and cans of sparkling water around."

"I had more than plenty." Grady nodded. "There was a whole pizza left—Braden said I should take it home. If that's okay. Tom said it would be."

"An entire pizza survived unscathed? I find that hard to believe." Philip laughed to settle Grady's quiet insecurity. He wished he had several more to send home with this kid. "Take home whatever's left. Tom knows what he's about."

Tom would have seen and recognized the same hunger; it'd been an intrinsic part of him when they'd met.

"Awesome, thanks. My little brothers will love that." Grady relaxed as the breeze and sounds of the others drifted over them. "This sure is a great backyard. Our trailer is on the other side of the valley, so for me it's open the back door and bam, side of a mountain."

"This backyard is a lot of why I wanted this house."

"That makes sense to me." Grady tapped his toes and then quickly said, "Coach told me you're a photographer? Really a photo… photojournalist."

"Coach is correct, I am one."

"That's so cool. And it's cool Coach picked here of all places to work on his project. We're all real glad your place was available and he didn't wind up in a cabin or something somewhere else. Don't you think?"

"I do," Philip could only agree. "Are you interested in photography?"

"I like sharing pictures and little movies on my socials. I've even cracked several thousand views on some of them." Grady smiled at that achievement and then shrugged. "Photography just seems like the, uh, more serious version of that."

"Makes sense. I'm pretty sure some of my publishers have used my photos on their socials, but I'm an old curmudgeon about that kind of thing, so I can't tell more than that."

Grady laughed. "That's legit. I've learned a lot from posting and reading how other people get their shots and stuff. But then Coach was telling me that you take great photographs that are famous, even. And that got me thinking about seeing, like, for-real good photographs and learning how and why people did those."

"It all has its place to tell the story of our world and lives, but that's a thoughtful and reasonable next step." Philip turned to Grady. "Do you want to come in and have a look at some of mine?"

Grady glanced down at his muddy self in horror. "Oh, no, sir. I don't think I can."

"I'm not getting any cleaner before I have to go in. It'll be fine. Besides, I can always make Coach mop up—it was basically his idea." Philip smiled and hooked an arm toward the house. He got to the sliding door and Grady remained at the edge of the patio, so he kicked out of his boots and said, "Just take your shoes off first."

That bit of caution and permission won Grady over into tiptoeing inside and through the house.

"You took all these?" he asked as he climbed the stairs.

"Almost all of them."

"Whoa."

Philip stayed in the foyer so Grady could look without feeling watched. He opened the front door to Zak and a cluster of kids, including Braden.

"Yo, Grady, you ready?" Braden yelled. He nodded at Philip. "Mr. C."

Quick as that, Grady forgot the photos. He thundered downstairs, shot out the door, said woops, and ran through the house to get his boots, and then he was panting slightly and standing with the others.

"The back looks amazing, guys. Thanks for your hard work," Philip said to the group. "I hope moving and getting big rocks in the ground really ups your football defense… skills." He waved his hands. "You know." They chuckled and then laughed differently when he added, "Someday one of you will have to tell me whose design it was, because it couldn't be Coach's."

"We actually had a good time!" Leif said.

Philip stayed on the top step as Zak walked them down the driveway to a neat line of cars, giving high-fives and good-jobs as they went. Braden and Grady with a few others went last, Braden at the wheel of an ancient but sturdy farm truck. Grady half lifted a box of pizza and waved at Philip, and then his attention was on whatever they talked about as they drove away.

Then only Tom and Kelly remained, and the house and yard seemed very quiet.

Zak approached Philip with a simmering grin. He climbed one step and reached out, tugged Philip to the edge of the higher step, framed Philip's face in his hands, and drew them into a long and lasting kiss.

"A bit delayed to finish our morning, but I'd say still good," Zak said after they parted.

"It'll do." Philip leaned in and kissed Zak again. "For now."

Zak pulled Philip into him and hummed contentedly.

"Not the best timing but the result—spectacular." Philip worked his hands under Zak's sweat-damp shirt so he could touch, skin to skin. "It really does look amazing."

"I'm happy you're happy." Zak set his cheek to Philip's and rocked them. "I'll have to see what else I can foist on those kids under the pretense of conditioning and team-building."

"Sounds good to me." Philip frowned. "When I'm more solvent again, I'll have to find work for Grady."

Zak tightened his hold. He understood.

"I can find work for Grady now," Zak offered.

Philip knew that's how it would be, and he sighed. It's not as if he'd make Grady wait—his shortfalls weren't the kid's fault. He wouldn't stop Zak and he couldn't resent it, but it wouldn't be the same as if he could have done so, immediately.

"That's true, and you should. Pay him with pizza but also be certain the cash stays his or goes to something he chooses."

Zak moved back to look at him. "Fair point and you're right. We'll do it." He kissed Philip's forehead softly. "All the boys are good kids, but Grady, he needs just a bit more attention. I knew you'd get it."

"Hard to miss."

"Not for some." Zak's jaw clenched.

Philip made an agreeing noise. He also knew that all too well. He kissed Zak's forehead, Zak's cheek, Zak's mouth, kept kissing until Zak's tension turned back to contentment and rising need.

"We should go check on Tom and Kelly," he said before they forgot themselves.

Zak blinked and then his eyes focused again. He got Philip under one arm but Philip pulled them sideways. He wanted to walk the path again.

"You're not wearing any shoes."

"My socks won't fall apart going to the patio."

Philip kept hold of Zak's hand and couldn't stop from grinning as they entered the shadowed and cool walk alongside the house. He held his other hand out to let the ferns tickle his fingers and noticed Zak doing the same.

"I like this," he said as they stepped around the house.

"I'm glad. Braden showed up with a truckload and two others, which was more than plenty to get from the patio to the overlook. I figured it'd be a shame to waste it."

"You figured well." Philip slipped from Zak's hand to tug his boots on.

Tom popped out the sliding door and waggled a thumb at the house. "Kelly's still snoozing but I got her shuffled to the couch." He grinned and held up a cooler. "To the victors the spoils."

Zak carried the cooler to the patio table and low whooped. Tom had loaded it with drinks the team shouldn't have. Philip nabbed a cider and walked to the overlook.

"Man, this is so great." Tom cracked open a beer. "When are you having us over for a bonfire?"

"Start one now," Philip said.

Tom considered the fire ring. "It's old to admit I'm too tired to bother, but I'm too tired to bother."

"Cheers, brother," Zak said in agreement.

They clacked bottles and watched the sunset, the night air mild and just short of chilly as the last chatter from the birds silenced into twilight. Philip thought, yes, very nice. He leaned against Zak and listened to them discuss getting Tom involved with the team and told himself don't get used to it.

Chapter Six

Philip yawned and it took hold so fully he shuddered all over. He poked the coffee pot awake and percolating and then stared muzzily across the house to the backyard. All night his tired eyes wouldn't stay closed, and even worn-out, his body wouldn't rest, so finally he'd slid from under the weight of Zak's arm and stepped to miss the creakiest stairs to go outside.

He sipped coffee and tasked his brain to think of things for Grady and whoever else showed up to do. Grady wasn't yet a constant presence at the house, but he and Zak had found plenty to keep the kid in chore money and meals. Braden usually came along, with the explanation that Grady didn't have a car, and from there a rotation of teammates.

Philip really did have some trees it'd be best to drop but he never mentioned that. Too dangerous for a couple of kids and two inexperienced adults to tackle, and he didn't want Zak to go and hire some company to do it. So they enlarged the garden beds, hauled rocks from the grade and riverbank, weeded, and built a small shed.

He let Grady grill him about photography and passed along an older DSLR he no longer used. Grady treated it like a precious thing, for his attention and listening more than the camera itself, always polite and grateful but starting to loosen up. Letting Grady talk him into setting up an account on the photo-sharing app he'd deftly avoided when suggested by various editors before then, and Grady being able to be his first follow, did even more.

When threads of icy blue lightened the horizon, he went inside.

He hadn't slept poorly in months—it was months since Zak had shown up. That seemed a milestone of some sort. As did how Philip had gotten used to Zak living with him. He'd been with Zak for longer than anyone else in any kind of arrangement.

He'd indulged in it and let it get away from him. No jobs, no writing, no reckoning. Philip still couldn't find fault in that, much as he tried. Or that Zak was too easy and appealing by half. But he should start to consider what next at some point. Soon.

Maybe tomorrow.

By rote he made a heap of flour and added ingredients for bread. He had a real knack for bread, and toast was one of his top comfort foods, so the recipe and actions had become muscle memory, almost innate. Zak hungrily chowing down with obvious enjoyment whatever loaf he baked and praising him after every bite only added to the pleasure of making it.

Philip had two mugs of coffee and the dough in a solid knead when he heard Zak on the stairs. The sound made him smile.

"Did I oversleep?" Zak asked as he wrapped around Philip from behind.

"Given we don't have a schedule, I don't see how."

"A compelling argument." Zak pushed in closer and watched Philip work for a while. Then he ground his hips to Philip's rear. "If I get my bread out and on the counter, would you knead it too?"

Philip spluttered and then laughed. "God that's… so awful. You're ridiculous." He dug into the dough and stretched it out for show. "And, yes. Absolutely I would."

"Okay, good." Zak lowered his arms to ring Philip's middle and rested his head on Philip's shoulder. "How about we have your bread for breakfast and then I take you to Barb's for eggs?"

"If we have breakfast here, why do we need to go out for breakfast?"

Zak kissed Philip's neck, once, again, and then again. "What, you don't like having second breakfast?"

"A compelling argument," he parroted, and turned into Zak's arms.

"Good morning," Zak said once they parted. "After eggs let's go to the farmer's market. The animal shelter is having a bake sale and there's something I want to show you."

Philip liked everything offered at the farmer's market and hated going, especially a weekend morning. Too many people with too much want for small talk.

"What if I do whatever you want to your bread instead?" He slipped his hands past Zak's waistband and settled his palms against the cut of Zak's hips.

Zak sucked in a breath and then squirmed away. "Ordinarily I'd hike you on a shoulder and right back to bed, but what I want to show you isn't promised to last. And the bake sale is today only." He shut his eyes when Philip's hands didn't relent. "How long until your bread is done?"

Philip leaned in and nipped Zak's chin. "Long enough."

Since the bread wasn't going to proof, he tossed it in a stoneware pan, shoved that into the oven, and then pushed Zak into the living room. He tugged a blanket onto the couch and shoved Zak to sit, snagging Zak's shirt and then lowering to kneel between Zak's legs.

Zak blinked heavily and cupped Philip's face in his hands, and his eyelids fluttered when Philip sucked on his thumb. He petted and combed Philip's hair and sighed, then his breath caught as Philip mouthed his nipples, his abs, and freed his cock.

Philip wasn't slow or gentle. He was ravenous. Zak stuttered when he squeezed and kept his grip tight, moaned when he stroked and then swallowed Zak nearly whole.

He'd learned exactly how Zak liked this—flick of tongue, twist of his hand, thumb pressed to the base of Zak's dick—and he pushed past that, pushed Zak to want and endure and then give him more. Zak kept hold of his face, and when Philip moaned encouragement and purposefully swallowed, Zak's fingers flexed and then curled, and Zak began fucking his mouth. Almost too hard, almost choking him, achy and drooling nonstop and perfect.

The first few times Philip did this, Zak had been careful, almost restrained. Zak's cock was as intoxicatingly large as the rest of him, nearly more than Philip could fit even using his throat, but it hadn't taken him long to intuit Philip wanted and needed some force and demand and sensation to be felt hours later, and restraint had given way to sweet intensity and hard pleasure.

Zak grunted and took himself in hand, hips jerking in needy bursts, and he tugged the corner of Philip's mouth with a thumb to open it wider.

Philip moaned approvingly and flattened his tongue. He met Zak's heated, determined gaze, and pushed his fist to the base of Zak's cock and tilted his head to let Zak finish as wanted, using him.

He watched Zak's grimace and furiously stroking hand and solar plexus moving in fierce contraction and knew Zak was so close. Zak cupped the back of his head and lifted off the couch in a half stand, and Philip's eyes leaked thin, fast-coursing tears when Zak pushed deeper and then the heat of Zak's completion filled him, the sound of Zak, the salty taste the burst of his own satisfaction at Zak's surrender.

Philip straightened from a low crouch intent on quickly getting off, but Zak sat heavily and grappled Philip with him, onto the couch, his lap, and then up on his knees, and got hold of both of Philip's arms. He manacled both of Philip's wrists in one hand and stroked Philip with the other.

Zak chuckled and Philip realized he'd babbled before moaning, loudly. Then Zak moaned as he stroked and worked Philip's cock into his mouth.

Philip almost shouted.

Beyond some small, experimental kisses and licks, Zak hadn't done this for Philip. He was hot and ready to come just from seeing Zak's lips around him—from Zak eagerly trying to swallow more. From Zak doing it at all.

He got his arms freed and gripped Zak's shoulders. Philip fought the instinct to hump Zak's face and the effort made him shake. Zak cupped his balls and then reached back to rub his hole hard and fast.

"I'm… you…" was the best Philip could do as a warning.

Zak shifted his grip to dig both thumbs into Philip's hips and held on, controlling Philip's movement but otherwise didn't flinch or redirect. He swallowed—tried to—when Philip did shout and then managed to catch Philip's collapse.

Philip landed on Zak's shoulder and panted. Fire erupted on his skin and then calmed under Zak's caresses until he could raise his head and lick Zak's neck and face clean. Then Zak pulled him into a kiss, and the kiss turned into sated quiet as they drifted and dozed.

He sort of returned to awareness when something chirped. It took a minute but then he remembered—the bread.

Zak had hold of him and his knees ached and his feet were numb and tingling. Zak might have drooled on his chest and they were sticky and their embrace overwarm and everything felt amazing. Zak guided him close to be kissed, slowly and methodically and full, at last gentled down.

The timer beeped again so Philip braced his hands on Zak's shoulders, winced as he shifted, and then wobbled off the couch. Zak steadied his legs and gave his tummy a quick kiss as he untangled from his pants and managed to stand. Philip stayed, swaying, stroking Zak's hair with Zak's cheek rested to his hip.

"Butter? Honey? Marmalade?" he croaked when the timer insisted a reminder.

"Yes please," Zak muttered, reluctantly letting go as Philip stepped back.

Philip thirstily gulped tap water as he washed up, and then he lobbed a wet rag into the living room. Zak yelped when it landed with a distinctive slap, and he grinned.

Then he tore the bread in manageable hunks and threw them and several spreads on the cutting board. Zak smiled, took and drained the glass of water Philip offered, squirmed to get into the corner of the couch, and pulled Philip to sit between his legs. Philip balanced the cutting board on his lap. It didn't take long for them to demolish the entire loaf, best eaten hot and both of them famished.

Philip rested into the curve of Zak's body and nuzzled his neck. "Still want to go?"

"After all that, I'm gonna need some eggs. And bacon. Definitely some kind of smoothie. But it's okay if you stay put or only want to go to Barb's."

Zak wasn't demanding or even disappointed, and that made the thought of saying no mostly to avoid a small-town crowd worse. He also kind of wanted to go.

"No, there's something you want to show me and hopefully the bake sale has lemon bars." Philip stretched and then rolled off the couch. "I'll go get ready—no joining me, though, if you really do want to go."

Zak grabbed the cutting board and then shooed him along. He had a quick shower and got dressed to Zak's showering, and then they met in the foyer.

They didn't linger at Barb's, but she was glad to see them. Zak ate a mountain of food and Philip only slightly less, and then Zak finished what he couldn't eat. Zak kept their knees pressed together under the table and ordered him extra lemon curd and opened the door as they came and went. It amused Philip and enchanted him, just a little.

"That hit the spot," Zak said as he climbed into the truck. "Should even tide me over until lunch." Barb's was on the opposite end of town from the farmer's market, and Zak covered Philip's thigh with a hand as they drove. How easily they fell in together, were with each other.

Philip counted Zak's knuckles with his fingertip. "For never doing this, you sure caught on quick. And you were right about not freaking out." He decided it was okay to add, "That's not true for everyone."

"No, it couldn't be, could it." Zak tightened his hand and then shrugged. "There's no explanation other than it's how I'm wired. I find what I like, go after what I want, and never feel shame or the need to apologize. I mean, I have my moments and my doubts same as anyone, but if it's good for me and doing no harm, I see no reason not to have it."

"I think being this innately well-adjusted is probably bad for you," Philip said dryly, and Zak laughed.

He also didn't care what people thought, but that mostly stemmed from learning how to navigate and then make a life without approval or permission that even if sought he wouldn't have gotten. First to survive, after that spite, and these days long comfortable in who he was.

"I'm a fast study when it's something I'm interested in." Zak flashed his crooked grin. "Besides, I have all the same parts and know what feels good and figured that gave me plenty to go on. And—" He killed the engine and lowered his voice. "—you're very vocal and responsive about what you like."

Philip bristled. "Am I? Isn't that convenient."

No one else had ever said as much, and the idea that Zak could and did read him easily was evident in all they did. But it also made him exposed and vulnerable, and in the moment, he didn't welcome that. He popped the door but Zak had hustled around to meet him, so he had to finish sliding to the ground and stood there with no immediate escape.

"For the record, it's not convenient at all. In fact, it's colossally inconvenient."

Philip made an unimpressed noise.

"The day the team helped with the pavers and I slipped my hand under your shirt? You did this little encouraging lean and lip lick that I've learned could turn into something real good real quick, and yes, I'm enjoying mentoring those kids, but no they do not need to know that much about me in sudden graphic technicolor."

Philip could easily imagine what he'd allow Zak to do after inviting such a kiss and what it'd lead to, and couldn't pretend he wouldn't be wholly distracted. Even in front of a football team.

"Ah, well, put it that way."

"Also for the record, hearing and watching what you like is what *I* like. Feel me?" Zak waggled an eyebrow but softened as he leaned in to kiss Philip. Light, a connection and tease, mouth to forehead.

Zak's admission had equal vulnerability, honesty, and it was silly but it settled him, righted exposure into something shared. He opened his eyes to Zak staring.

"Am I doing it again or something?" he asked without thinking.

"No. But I am resisting kissing you again, and gauging that bundling you right back up in the truck wouldn't be that difficult, and thinking about how fast I could make the drive home."

"Gotcha, so. Normal everyday stuff."

"These days? Yes," Zak said without shame or conceit. "But to all that, I do have a confession to make."

Philip nodded, go on.

"I was attracted to you from the jump, first talking at the house and then during dinner, and after I admitted that, I found I was okay with it. New, but okay, although I almost didn't go through with coming to stay."

Philip's small noise of protest came unbidden and Zak smiled.

"Almost, but I couldn't resist. The house, the easiness I feel there, you. Then it only got worse—good worse, considering. I was touch and go there for a few days, though. But...." Zak considered his words. "I expected it to fade, especially the morning after the tension broke. That's usually how it goes for me. But how it's going with you is, the more I have you the more I want you." He almost glared at Philip. "That's *not* how it usually goes for me."

Hectic blood bolted into Philip's cheeks and heated his core. "How long to drive home?" He sounded breathless.

"Is it indecent exposure if no one can see you?" Zak asked against Philip's cheek.

Philip could tell Zak meant to tease but his voice was rough, his breathing likewise harsh.

"I'm so good with this in part because I can't get enough. That and I'm happy—the house, the easiness there with you, you—makes wanting and having it seem simple."

Philip didn't know if those were declarations or promises, and he wasn't ready to ask outright or allow himself any. But it sounded like plenty to keep going on for a while. Like three months more and not overthink it.

"The same could be said for me," Philip did admit. "On all counts." He tightened his grip and realized he had tight hold of Zak's hips.

They stared at each other under the protective shade of a low-boughed tree, noise of the market seeming far away, until the crunch of tires and hammer of several car doors interrupted uncomfortably close.

Zak groaned and spun away. "C'mon, let's go get lots of goodies to help some fuzzy faces and look at chairs. Henry said he'd have two for sure at the market today."

Philip was annoyed and chilled and vibrated with disappointment. Really his own fault—their fault—standing in a damn parking lot, forgetting everything except each other while admitting to unending horniness. He rolled his shoulders and then regained his bearings, reached behind his seat, shoved a few neatly folded bags into his pocket, and got moving to pursue Zak's lengthening stride.

"Philip! My man," Tom called from the opposite corner of the parking lot.

Philip waved and walked to meet Tom in the middle.

"You're looking a bit dazed. Is everything all right?"

"It's early and I'm still warming up, but everything's fine." Philip ignored the urge to add a loosening hitch in his step.

"Fine, and yet you're here? I thought you despised the farmer's market."

"No, I just don't particularly enjoy the throng."

"It's maybe two-dozen people."

"Like I said." Philip surveyed the bustling green the town had converted to a park and general-use space well before his time.

Tom's parents had brought them to some outdoor concerts over the years and there was a seasonal booth with caramel apples and apple bread and applesauce all to die for, but he preferred making an order and picking that up.

"Heh, I see why you're here." Tom pointed at Zak, who hadn't made it past the first stall and already had a handful of goodies, a head taller than everyone and everyone laughing at something he'd said.

"He's criminally friendly. Never met a stranger or something like that. But apparently there's some chairs I must see, and the guy selling the chairs wouldn't hold them." He wasn't sure that was accurate but, close enough.

"Wait. You're at the farmer's market first thing on a Sunday cozy with Mr. Exactly Your Type shopping for chairs?" Tom howled with laughter and slapped Philip's back. "Oh my fucking fuck."

Philip lurched forward and then turned around incredulously. "What was that for?"

"Hah!" Tom pointed at Philip. "I knew you were attracted to Zak. I knew it. I'm not sure I expected you to move this fast, given all your protestations but—phew. Move you did."

"Whatever."

"Philly, Cheesesteak, bestie…." Tom raised his eyebrows and leaned in expectantly.

Philip rolled his eyes. "You haven't called me that since freshman year."

"And I haven't seen you this bone-deep satisfied since maybe sophomore year when you actually dated that chem major." Tom shrugged. "Keep denying it, like I wasn't standing here watching you watch him, all big-eyed and gooey."

"Gooey? I'm not gooey. I don't do *gooey*."

"An excellent dodge attempt, but I'm not fooled. So, by my expert deductions, that means if you don't do gooey, then you did do him."

"Deductions?" Philip rubbed his temple and said with exaggerated grievance, "Why are you like this." He realized he was watching Zak, still. Sunlight on blond hair, confident but disarming smile, loose limbed, charming with genuine interest in everyone else. There really was no denying it, at least not to Tom. "I should probably end it soon. Well—it's only six months anyway. I don't have to trust it past that."

"I dunno man, sometimes what you see is what you get. And I'm inclined to believe that about your guy."

"My guy?"

Tom beamed. "Exactly." He shoved Philip to get them moving.

Philip grunted but started walking. "What gave me away? Aside from you being a complete weirdo. Unless you were bluffing, and now I have to be doubly irritated with you."

"Little things add up. Like how you left the house in an awful hurry after playing footsie over cheesecake bites with Zak practically pushing you out the door. Then you got awfully quiet in our little besties chat and have been dodging dinner invites from me *and* Kelly. And now I see you here, in the actual early morning, looking… well." Tom rubbed his thumb and two fingers together. "Also, as we've established, I know you. That simple." He glanced at Zak. "That simple and your guy there keeps checking on where you are and is practically fit to burst, strutting like a boasting banty rooster."

"Does he?" Philip was unaccountably gratified by that, although he couldn't see what Tom claimed.

"The man isn't hiding that he likes you, there's that much." Tom spread his hands in front of them. "I was once a trial lawyer, remember. Hell, just being a lawyer means you should learn how to read people."

"Second time this morning I've been told I give myself away. And this after a lifetime of being impossible to read. Inscrutable. Maybe even sphinxlike."

"You definitely have some cat qualities. Kelly also suspects." Tom shouldered sideways into him. "It's only people who really know and understand you. Take it as a compliment—a positive, even."

"I can try, but I don't have to be gracious about it."

"That's never your worry. But look, it'll be fine. The clock is already ticking, you're gonna save your house, and he's a good guy. Lord knows what he sees in you, but that part's not my business." Tom nodded. "Not to get too gooey myself about it, but I'm glad you went for it. You needed something good after all the crap that's happened. And something distracting."

Zak looked around and then found Philip and smiled. Philip wouldn't deny it, and for today, wouldn't regret it.

"Ya know what, you asshole, I did."

Tom gave him a satisfied nod but then frowned. "The downside is now I'm going to have to find a way to warn a good buddy off hurting you."

"You just said it'd be fine and he's a good guy. And—please don't."

"I did and he is, but it's best friend duty stuff. Codes and honor bound and all that."

"Well, I hereby free you of that obligation." Philip shook his head. "And from having any sort of talk like this for another say, two years."

Tom clicked his tongue twice. "I'll add it to my calendar."

"Great, I will try to be out of the country. And now, I guess I need to see a man about some chairs."

"I already loaded up on anything pecan or cherry and should really get my haul back to the house." Tom started trotting away, stopped, and then said, "Come over for dinner soon, any day is fine. Bring your guy." He grinned at Philip's expression and then waved as he left.

Philip made his way to his guy and who he assumed was Henry. Not that he'd had anything specific in mind for a Henry who had chairs, but someone maybe younger than him with a waxed and curled mustache, dressed in fawn work overalls and a dress shirt, and covered in tats hadn't been what he'd expected. He appreciated the style, though.

"There he is," Zak said as Philip approached. "Philip, Henry. Henry, Philip gets final say on the chairs."

Henry stuck out a beefy hand. "Philip, glad to meet you and take your time."

The chairs were long but low profile, thin slats of teak with cedar inlay made dark and smooth with oil, modern lines that gave them a naturalistic appearance rather than seeming cold.

"Let me demonstrate the mechanism." Henry lifted a wooden yoke attached to the chair back, and then fit it into successive notches that increased the recline as he went.

Philip tried it at Henry's wordless suggestion and easily set the chair at a near upright position. "These are beautiful. You do some damn fine craftsmanship."

"Thanks so much, I really appreciate that. Zak told me you're also an artist and build furniture, so that means a lot to hear."

"I'm a hack compared to you. Mine's mostly live edge or simple cuts and then shellacking basically how I find it."

Henry nodded. "I do live edge too. And hey, we have to start somewhere. Come to the shop sometime and we can talk techniques. I've gotten to almost all dovetail or wood bore fastenings I make myself, and using reclaimed wood," Henry said with evident pride.

"I think I'd enjoy seeing the shop." Philip meant it beyond polite chit-chat. "And reclaimed wood explains the subtly differing tones, I'd guess?"

"Yes, exactly. Bit of this, bit of that in each of them, even though it's the same species." Henry patted a chair. "Give one a sit, have a short nap, whatever you like. I'll check with you in a bit, but no rush."

Philip nodded but his attention got caught by the pricing menu on a nearby table. He went over and picked it up and then stared to be sure he read it correctly. Zak stood expectantly for his reaction but he had no words, nothing other than a stunned shake of his head. He shot out from Henry's booth and wound up in the shelter of an enormous oak tree near the center of the green.

"Those are way too expensive," he hissed as Zak joined him. Zak started to argue but he said incredulously, "A few of those is a good chunk of my property taxes. And that's way too much, you can't spend that much on m—on chairs."

Philip hadn't felt this particular spike of anxiety in years. That big of an expense always meant things were unsafe. A debt they'd have to drop everything to outrun. A car he couldn't fix and a replacement he couldn't afford. A burial that might have cost him his house.

That had to be what drove his reaction. Dredged up memories and confronting another loss because of her and then Zak, wonderful and so *nice* and able to buy his only security from under him without a second thought.

But he trusted Zak. Standing there knowing Zak had only the best intentions told him as much with sudden clarity. But lifelong precarity clung as a persistent shadow. Mistrust of what got leveraged after guilt gifts or to subtly manipulate when he'd been too young to realize the price attached couldn't be banished by intimate mornings and breakfast out and a pleasant sunny day.

"Shit." Zak let out a breath and waited a beat. "You're listening?"

"Sure." Philip made a go-on motion at Zak's look. The fever in his brain had already cooled. "Seriously, I am listening."

"I can afford a lot. To be blunt, almost anything at this point. Those chairs will barely be a blip for me." Zak raised Philip's hand and flattened it to his chest. "But I'm sorry I sprung that on you. It didn't even occur to me to consider them in anything other than my means. But seriously, whatever I get—for me, for the house, for you—I'll never make you pay for it. In any way."

It didn't surprise Philip that Zak got it, almost exactly. But it chagrined him and he wished he'd buried the reaction and said *sure whatever, good, get the chairs.* He released a long, controlled exhale.

"No, I'm sorry. The thing is…." Philip's thoughts quieted and the place beneath Zak's warm hand ached. He didn't admit things often and resented the aftermath of what felt like oversharing, but Zak didn't deserve to be lumped into guilt gifts or worse, or to feel likened to that. "So, I suck at this because I don't care about explaining myself to people but you're not, uh, people."

Zak quirked a smile at that.

"It's been an up and down few months to now, so pretty sure my reaction was cumulative. And I'm good these days, but being raised less than poor and fighting to stay escaped from that did its lasting damage.

And sometimes it still shows. That and, well, for so long unexpected gifts came with a price. I'm overreacting because I didn't want...."

"You didn't want that to also be me. Even if rationally that wasn't what knocked you sideways."

Philip nodded and closed his eyes and next he knew, he was folded into a tight hug, and not worried or unhappy to be there. Zak held him, unconcerned at being in the middle of everything, and then moved to grip his shoulders at arm's length and give him a thorough study.

"How about we agree we both just had a big whoops, hey sorry, but no big deal. I'm not offended, you're allowed to feel things, even irrational things sometimes, we're all okay. Okay?"

"Yes, okay. That actually sounds great. Particularly if we can agree to just move on."

"Only if you are actually fine."

"Promise." Philip continued to hate having done this but that was his issue, and it wasn't regret for just telling Zak what was up. He scrubbed his eyes and huffed shortly. "Geez, what a morning. This just proves me correct in being wary of the farmer's market."

"I outright enjoy it but have no trouble saying home is better." Zak massaged Philip's shoulders, and the intensity in his eyes cleared. "The chairs are super amazing, though, right? I like them but I also thought you'd love them."

"You got me there." Philip chewed on his lip.

"We don't have to get any."

"So, after everything, this feels a bit gauche to say but... I want four of them. Two for the patio—"

"—two for the overlook." Zak laughed. "All right, then, let's get the truck and get four. Henry brought six."

Philip settled into relief and a smile and let it go. He followed after Zak and said expansively, "Oh, he knows what he's doing."

Zak wound up buying all six, leaving Henry mildly dazed and incredibly stoked. Philip used it as a rare opportunity to try and enjoy an actual splurge and not calculate how many dinners he could get out of ramen packs and canned vegetables or try to outwit any repercussions attached.

They found two fit on the patio and two fit on the overlook, but anything more made both areas seem crammed or unbalanced, and the rest of the yard overtaken by natural planting and the path made no ready spots for either.

"How about these for the farm?" Zak finally asked after they'd dragged the two orphan chairs to the patio for the millionth time.

"I like that idea, and Tom should be home by now. But let's just do it because if we take a break I won't want to get moving again."

"Agreed."

They loaded up and secured the chairs and soon were rumbling the familiar route to the farm. Zak reached over and laced their fingers together, circling his thumb in Philip's palm and humming a nondescript tune as he drove.

Philip rolled his window down and rested his head back and concentrated on the push of the wind and the slow rasp of Zak's touch.

Zak reversed from the driveway to park in the lawn, where the front door widened into a huge side deck. They turned to each other and without thought, Philip smiled. Zak kissed his fingertips and held on, sat a minute, and then let go to get going. Philip hopped from the truck as Tom barreled out of the house. He could hear Kelly inside. Crying.

"What happened?"

Tom threw up his hands. "I said something about a cradle, and now apparently everything is ruined and our kid won't graduate college and will fail to flourish because their first night home won't be in it."

"But you already have a crib, we built it."

"Yes, but this is different—it's an old cradle, the one I slept in my first night home."

Philip nodded slowly. "Okay, so, how about we get that one set up? That doesn't seem too difficult."

"He doesn't even remember where it is," Kelly said as she clomped onto the porch. "He could barely describe it. How can we follow family tradition if he doesn't know what it looks like?" she wailed.

"Family tradition?" Philip closed his eyes and chased a memory until it became a picture. "That one made of walnut, the sides are wood-turned spindles, and it hangs on a matching standing frame from fancy wrought iron rings. Right?" He sketched it in the air as he spoke.

"That does sound right." Tom flattened his palm toward the ground. "About yea-high, aged dark brown. I think Mom said it was Great-Grandma's."

"Your great-grandma's? That far back?" Kelly's upset threatened to veer into peeved.

Philip shot a warning glare at Tom to not say whatever was about to pop off. "It used to be in my room. Your mom kept old quilts and stuffed animals in it, and then one day it was gone. She told me she'd moved it so I could have more space."

"Your room?" Zak asked.

"After Tom kept dragging me here and I kept showing up, his parents designated a bedroom as mine."

Philip remembered how it'd looked, only his third visit, when Tom's mom had shown him the empty dresser and chest of drawers and bookcase he was instructed to use however he preferred. She'd marched him to a closet and had him choose bedding, a quilt, and then a few items from around the house. He'd hung some of his own photos in there and kept a box of stuff from college through the years that'd stayed in a corner until he bought his house.

"The one you wouldn't stay in when your house was gutted." Tom crossed his arms, clearly still irritated about that.

"Your office was plenty comfortable. And I told you, it's different being a dumb college kid to intruding on your grown-up life." Philip cut his hands in front of him. "Whatever, that's not the point. The point is, yes, it's an old cradle, yes, baby's first night home is a family tradition, and it's in the barn."

"What? Where? I went and looked."

Philip turned to Tom. "Did you look or did you open the big door, stand there and give things a once-over, not see it immediately, and call it done?"

Tom huffed instead of answering, which told Philip everything. Kelly had started to cry again. He let out a slow breath.

"We brought you something, and they're great but unwieldy. So Tom, how about you help us get them from Zak's truck, and Kelly, you can decide where you want them. While you do that, Zak and I will find the crib—I know just where to look. A plan?"

"A plan," Zak said cheerily and strolled to his truck.

They did exactly that and then Philip tugged Zak to the barn in hasty retreat, Kelly crying over Zak's generosity and the surprise and Philip knowing about the cradle, Tom glad to be busy measuring areas on the wide back deck and in the lawn as potential chair homes.

The dogs had hung back but romped with them through the yard and darted inside as Philip pulled a side door open to loll in the smells and old sawdust and new hay.

He flipped on the lights and stood there.

"Do you actually know where it is?"

Philip laughed. "Fuck no. But I wasn't about to say that to Kelly, and I do know Molly wouldn't have gotten rid of it. Since it's not with her or in the house, it's gotta be in here. No clue why they didn't simply text her, but I'm also not in the middle of a baby meltdown."

"So it's just a matter of finding it. Quickly as we can."

"Pretty much." Philip walked along, studying various piles and shelves, and eventually decided on the tidy stack of boxes in the far corner. "This enormous thing used to be a cattle barn—they'd walk the girls up the dirt ramp at the back, there." He pointed to the huge bay doors that didn't really roll open anymore. "Tom's granddad knocked out the stalls, and his dad used it as a workshop. Tom considered renovating it to be the law offices."

"I think the building in town is better."

"Much. This is an amazing space—as a barn. Turning it into offices would cost a fortune. And ruin the barn. Also, Tom and Kelly can walk across the square to court so why bother." Philip poked at a wide box that turned out to be disapprovingly shallow. "This is the oldest remaining intact barn in the county, and still has the original, and first, cattle ramp that got built three-counties wide. Tom should probably get it on some historical register."

"How do you know all this?"

Philip shrugged. "Whenever I was here, I'd sit at the kitchen table, Molly and Ben would talk, and I'd listen."

"That sounds great."

Zak meant that and Philip appreciated the sincerity and understanding. Zak would think it great, but also seemed satisfied it happened for him.

"It was great. So is Molly's cooking, and she always had containers of cookies or rolls or bread out, making the table the place to be."

"They had a room for you almost immediately, didn't they." Zak removed the top layer of boxes. "Does this cradle break down into parts?"

"Not the main section, which is probably three by five, but the frame does. And yes, they did. I think Molly took one look at me and my fate was decided."

"Good," Zak said firmly, sounding ready to send Molly flowers or something.

Philip smiled into the tall box he searched. "This all looks like stuff from the house Molly thought the kids might want someday, so I'm thinking we're on the right track." He tapped his fingers on the sides and frowned.

Zak had discovered a stack of photos, and something had caught his attention to shuffle through them. "Whoa, you're so young. And appear to be half-starved." He twirled one of the pictures to clasp under a finger facing Philip.

He and Tom were on the porch as Philip remembered the farm, faded and worn but solid and welcoming. They stood arm-in-arm wearing shirts in reverse colors bearing their college initials, and the mascot was made whole if they matched the shirtfronts together.

"God, we thought those shirts were awesome. That's our freshman year and my first visit here, making me young and definitely starved." Philip remembered being hungry and wary and defensive back then—he didn't realize how clearly it showed, how hollow-eyed and gaunt he'd been.

Zak scowled.

"A lot happens in a decade. I'm all good now. Molly fattened me up, and I haven't looked back."

"Well, someone damn should have." Zak waved the pack of photos. "Think I could smuggle these home to look at?" He paused. "Would that be okay with you?"

"Totally fine." Philip mused, "I don't have any pictures from then except those I took, and they're all moody and terrible and artistic. And Tom will let us have them outright, no sneaking required. Especially if we bring back the dorkiest ones to make fun of."

"Nice." Zak stood motionless for a thoughtful moment and then let out a long breath. "You never dated or messed around with Tom, did you?" He said it like he already knew.

"Did you ask Tom?"

"No, I just can tell. I think."

Philip lifted the lid on a box but let it fall again so he could look at Zak. "Nope, never dated, never anything. It was never even a question. Tom and I clicked immediately—as friends and nothing more."

"I shouldn't be glad about that or admit that I'm glad about that, but I'm very glad about that."

"I don't mind." Philip smiled, and then after several minutes he asked, "Why did you break up with the woman who offered on the house with you?"

"I offered on the house," Zak emphasized. He piled boxes they'd been through and set them aside. "We sorta dated. She actually chased me to Toronto, got mad when I didn't change plans and still left the next day, got madder when I kept to a road trip with pokey and obscure sightseeing along the way instead of chartering a flight, and was incandescent with rage I wanted to buy some terrible little house in the sticks."

"Wow. I shouldn't sarcastically say 'what a charmer' but, incredibly sarcastically, what a charmer."

Zak laughed. "As I said, we sorta dated. Which was fine until it wasn't. And then I found the house—and you—and it's as if it was all waiting for me."

Philip liked that more than he wanted to admit. It seemed more right than he could afford to believe.

"If that's the case, why'd you wait so long to come back?"

"I had some things to wrap up and also told myself I was being needlessly impulsive. But then those things were wrapped up and I still had the listing of the house in an open tab on my phone. I more or less showed up the next day."

"And now look at you."

"Couldn't be happier." Zak spread his arms and then sneezed as barn dust billowed. He sneezed again and braced against an ancient refrigerator box that jostled hollowly from his weight. He slid it free from its row and walked into a cleared spot. "Hey, check it. Three by five would fit in here on its end. And it's not heavy."

They tilted and then tabled it to lower to the floor. Philip untucked the flaps and peered inside. Something bulky of a promising shape wrapped in old sheets beckoned. He pulled while Zak held on to the box, and then he had the sheets undone and the cradle revealed.

"Not even dusty," he said and patted the top rail. "I didn't want to mention that Molly did trash the old mattress, but that shouldn't be hard to replace."

"Or just use blankets or something."

"Plenty of those to go around." Philip shuffled forward to half crawl into the box and hand Zak pieces of the frame and then the legs.

"That has to be all the parts, but we're missing some hardware." Zak went to the far end of the fridge box and lifted. Nothing jangled or slid out. "Did you see anything taped to the inside?"

"Nope." Philip returned to a box he'd set aside. "This has baby books and stuff, so it'd make sense to pack them together."

"Reasonable. I'm guessing I-bolts and nuts for the frames and then a set of hooks to hang the actual crib from." Zak measured the hardware opening on the frame's legs with his thumb and forefinger and held that up for reference. "Yup just, push the bolt in there, and that'll tie the leg and base together, and then tighten with a nut."

Philip dug past albums and cutesy padded books, lifting and separating and sort of bracing things with his elbows to see the bottom layer. Several food tins—crackers, cookies, tea, chocolate—and he worked them free. One rattled, and he grinned at Zak and passed it over.

"Voila." Zak dumped the fastenings into his hand.

"Thank Christ and thank you, Molly," Philip muttered as he worked everything back in. The corner of an album caught a packet and it lifted, so he shook the box, but instead of settling, it sailed over the top and whapped on the floor. "Great," he said and awkwardly reached for it, not quite able to let go of the box as he got the packet under two fingertips, and scrabbled it under his palm.

He tossed the packet on top and started shutting the flaps, and then creeping recognition stilled him. Philip didn't want to know that handwriting, to untie the string on the packet, to confront what was in these few envelopes.

"What's up?"

Philip whipped around to face Zak. He'd been miles and years and memories away. Zak had the crib put together and Philip couldn't account for that. It'd been only a moment. He held four envelopes in a fan and clutched a letter in his fist.

"Everything good?"

He wanted to burn the letters immediately, read and reread them, punish himself by painstakingly learning what she'd said. They warmed his hands and gut in a sickly way, and he had insane thoughts that tucking them in a pocket or taking them into the farmhouse—or his house—would be inviting the dark entropy of her ghost in with them.

"I'm fine," he said levelly. "Just surprised that some of the things Molly kept were mine, and it's weird seeing them. I wonder why she did."

And why had his mother written to Molly. Worse, he had every idea and despised all of them.

"You're important to her and she probably thought those things would be important to you someday. Or she wanted them for her own memories and reference." Zak wrapped a gentle hand around Philip's fist. "Lots of reasons."

Zak kept hold as if to make sure Philip relaxed, so he stuffed the letter back in the envelope, folded all four in a bundle, and unconcernedly tossed them in the box.

"Sure you're all right?" Zak stroked the bridge of Philip's nose.

"Yes, it's just—strange déjà vu or something. You know."

"Even suddenly unearthing good stuff you haven't thought about in years is jarring. The rush of memories and feelings associated with it all, and then having to let it go quiet again." Zak kissed Philip. "I get it."

Philip hooked his hand around Zak's neck for another kiss. He didn't want to talk about it anymore, and he needed the memories to go quiet. Demanding a deeper, longer kiss distracted them both. When Zak kept it controlled, he added tongue, then teeth, then the insinuation of his thighs against Zak's groin.

Zak made a low noise and gripped the back of Philip's shirt, then tugged to get his hands underneath. Philip rolled his hips and Zak spun them so he was pushed against a post and then lifted up.

"Uh, hey, guys."

They sprang apart, Philip almost eating dirt and Zak rocking before grabbing the post. Zak grabbed him and then left a hand on Philip's back.

"Anyway," Tom said loudly and shook his head. "Did you find it?"

"Yes, and got it together too." Zak's intonation was normal, but his voice was thick and ragged.

"We were just about to bring it in." Philip cleared his throat. He sounded no better.

"Sure, whatever. Can we get it in now? Kelly's water just broke."

Chapter Seven

Philip dropped his end of the cradle and went to intercept Kelly's agitated walk on the concrete pad in front of the garage when she doubled over.

"Tom's getting the go bag and the car out, so let's go this way," he coaxed and stayed with her as she duck-walked, hands on knees, and then huffed shortened breaths.

"My mom isn't here yet," she cried. "Oh, ouch. Owie ouch ouch this sucks."

Philip got her moving again. "Did you text her that it's happening?"

Kelly winced and nodded, and her grip on his arm became a vise.

"Then safe to say half the Bronx is being mobilized as we speak. She and your Pops will be here soon."

"That's true and they will." Kelly's eyes watered, half tears and half pain. "Thanks for finding the cradle."

"We both know Tom's useless at stuff like that. I can't even list the many, obvious things he couldn't find in a tiny dorm room—it's almost a talent."

"And you saved me marching out there to do it myself and birthing my baby in a barn." Kelly groaned and bent forward again.

"Here's Tom," Zak said from behind them. He more or less carried Kelly to the car and deposited her inside with a quick peck on her cheek. "No speeding, and keep us updated."

Philip looked in past Zak. Tom was probably paler than Kelly.

"You got this," he said to Tom with a confident nod, and extracted his arm from Kelly's hold. "So do you." He squeezed her hand, and then both he and Zak stepped away.

Zak closed the door and thumped the roof, and Tom peeled off in a tight turn and slowed to not-quite-barreling as he neared the road. They watched until the car was out of sight and then carried the cradle inside.

"I figured Kelly as someone with everything planned to the nth and ready to go," Zak said as they surveyed the chaos in the house.

"You figured right, but the baby's about two weeks early."

"Ah, that'd do it."

"Do you mind hanging out while I clean?" He couldn't let them come home to this.

"Do you mind if I take dish duty and you get stuff put away? Dishes are straightforward—you know the house."

"Deal."

Philip's sweep of the house didn't take long as the mess was superficial. He returned to the kitchen as Zak started the dishwasher and directed where larger, dried items belonged.

"Cradle upstairs?"

"Yup." Philip had dragged it into the living room and tidying gave him an idea. "It needs a mattress, but the nearest big box store isn't close and not like delivery will arrive tomorrow. And while I've no idea when they'll send Kelly home, I do know the minute they get here, she'll want to use the cradle. There's at least seven pet beds in this house, and the dogs don't use any of them. In fact…" He sped to the garage, found one he remembered stowing for Kelly some months ago still in its shrink wrap, and brought it inside. "Cut that in half and it's the right size."

"Close enough." Zak ripped the plastic away and unzipped the cover. "Stiff foam. Bread knife?"

Philip nodded. "Bread knife."

They butchered the foam into a passable mattress, wrapped it in a fitted sheet and then the baby afghan Philip knew Kelly's mom had made, and laid a flannel pad on top. Then carried the cradle upstairs and left it at the foot of the bed.

"That'll do until Kelly gets something permanent. I'll remind Tom to get on it—pronto." Philip gave the cradle a gentle push and it swayed smoothly. "Nice."

Back downstairs and he went to a side door and whistled for the dogs. They destroyed their dinner in seconds, and he got them crated with chews and promises someone would check on them soon.

"Anything else?" Zak folded and draped a throw blanket on the sofa. "If not, let's go to dinner. I'm famished and too tired to think about cooking."

"Dinner sounds amazing." Philip stopped short. "Can you believe it was only this morning we got breakfast? Feels like a week ago, at least."

"And I just noticed it's dark outside. What a day." Zak came close to snag Philip's hips and slot them to his. "What are you in the mood for?"

Philip's pocket buzzed and they stilled. "Something takeout with enough for Tom." He blinked and then swallowed down momentary overwhelm. "She's here—the baby."

"That was fast, wow." Zak whooped and pulled Philip into a crushing hug. After a moment he pushed them apart. "Food, baby, let's get moving."

Driving a half hour to the larger town, Chinese takeout, and a milkshake for Kelly later had them pulling into the regional hospital and finding their way to the maternity ward. Tom met them in the hall and devoured an egg roll while sneaking them past the nurse's station.

"For the new momma," Zak said and set the milkshake on Kelly's tray table. "It's double chocolate."

"My heroes, once again." Kelly looked exhausted and elated. "Come say hello to Madeline Leigh."

Philip narrowed his eyes. "You guys are gross and I don't like you anymore."

"Liar." Tom laughed. Then he explained to Zak, "Philip's middle name is Lee. But for my baby girl it's Leigh." He spelled it out with emphasis on the *-igh*.

"Don't be ridiculous, you love it." Kelly ticked off her fingers as she said, "Mom is Maria, and then Tom's mom is Molly, so we thought another M-name was needed. Tom suggested Leigh and it's perfect."

"She didn't like Philly or Cheesesteak nearly as well."

"Cheesesteak?" Zak asked with far too much interest.

Tom held a hand to his mouth and said from behind it, "I'll tell you later."

Zak big-winked and nodded.

Philip rolled his eyes and walked around to the bassinet parked at Kelly's side. "Whoa. Look at this beautiful little burrito you guys made."

Madeline was as any baby—tiny, pink, wrinkled—but Madeline was Tom and Kelly's, so that made her completely different.

"Say hello to Uncle Philip," Tom whispered.

Her face scrunched and she made a tiny noise that kind of destroyed Philip, and he braved resting a hand on her belly.

"We told you it was a girl," he finally said.

"And I'm not complaining." Tom tugged her cap down. "We did good, huh?"

"Real good." Philip had anticipated caring about the baby, but he didn't expect it to be so profound or his attachment so immediate and easily given. "Congrats, you two. And Kelly, I can't be surprised at your continued efficiency but dang, you made fast work."

"Barely got me in the room and there she was," she said smugly and popped the top off the milkshake to eat with a spoon. "This is so good. Oh, and you were right, Mom and Pops are on their way."

"See? It all worked out."

Zak had hung back but Philip made space and motioned him over.

"And this is Uncle Zak," Kelly said, and something about that seemed so tangible and permanent.

Philip chalked it up to the heightened emotions of meeting a brand-new human, especially as Zak only smiled his usual crooked grin and tapped a fingertip on Madeline's nose.

"It's an honor to meet you, little bug."

Tom had dug into the food and arrayed it on an extra rolling tray table. Philip nabbed an egg roll before Tom could claim it, topped it on some lo mein, and sat with it and wonton soup in a distinctly uncomfortable chair. Tom perched on the bed and inhaled beef and broccoli. Zak loaded up on whatever was left and carefully lowered into the other chair.

"Thank you for this." Tom shoveled fried rice from the container into his mouth with chopsticks. "And did we thank you for the chairs? I don't think we did but honestly, it's all a blur."

"Consider them a baby gift." Zak stacked his containers and took Philip's. "They're perfect for long naps with Maddie."

"Maddie." Kelly smiled. "Nice. As are the chairs."

After they'd eaten, exhaustion hit.

Kelly fell asleep and Tom rested next to her as Zak yawned and zoned out. Philip crept from the room, found a cellphone-friendly waiting area two floors down, and made use of the strong signal to deal with a backlog of emails and messages.

He opened an email from a friendly colleague and blinked at the rate attached. Harriet needed a photographer only, would write the story, and hoped he was available. Philip wondered if he'd missed out—she'd sent the email two full days ago and needed to move on it quickly. Apparently she'd pitched a story a while ago and it'd been tabled until the major storm about to menace the East Coast roared to life.

Philip had no idea about the weather. It showed how removed—and indulged in being with Zak—he'd become. He browsed some prelims on the storm's forecast. The majority saw it scouring the coast and then hooking under New York's chin to head to sea, but the outlier model had it boring inland.

Philip liked working with Harriet, and the money made his mind up to accept. He couldn't let the gap in his active work continue to get so large it swallowed him.

Her responding email pinged minutes later. She couldn't wait to see him and would pick him up tomorrow evening, tickets and expenses paid. Philip cringed at the amount he charged to get from the nearest small airport to the one she'd collect him from, but at least wasn't his ultimate responsibility.

He triple-checked the flight and how long it'd take to drive to the airport; he could leave early in the morning and get one more night at home.

"Did anyone know there's a huge and potentially historic storm about to barrel up the coast?" he asked quietly as he entered Kelly's room.

Zak stirred when Philip spoke, stretched his legs and crossed them at the ankles, and nodded. "A few of the boys are excited at the prospect we might get some conditioning mornings rained out."

"From what I gather it's a hurricane that's not getting called one and is threatening several major urban centers." Tom patted Kelly's middle. "Good thing Maddie decided to show up early and her folks will be here safe and sound tomorrow."

"Well, I'm about to head into it." Philip stood.

"Assignment or on your own?" Tom asked.

"A last-minute invite, but for a solid reporter and paid well, which is mostly why I accepted. She's got some angle on profiling exclusive beachfront neighbors that are also disappearing beachfront neighborhoods." Philip glanced at Zak, who hadn't reacted.

"So not jumping aboard the NOAA plane and flying through the eye or gunning into it with some storm chasers?" Tom smirked. "You're getting soft."

Philip tutted. "I'd do either again in a heartbeat—but Harriet and her pitch is who called."

"How long will you be gone?" Zak stood and gathered the takeout leavings into the emptied paper bag.

"Not even a week, depending on how fast the storm moves." Philip went to get another look at Maddie and tell her goodbye.

"Spend the day at the farm when you get back. You can tell us about the story, and by then Maddie will have her eyes open for more than a minute at a stretch." Tom slid off the bed and met Philip at the foot to haul him into a hug.

Philip endured and hugged Tom back. "Congrats again—she's gorgeous and I'm not just saying that because you're my friend." He moved back and smiled. "And look, I was here after all."

"And we're glad for that." Tom clapped Philip's shoulders and then turned to Zak. "Thanks for being here too, bud. Much appreciated."

Zak started their complicated high-five and bro-hug routine, and then they crept from the room, crammed trash from dinner into a can in the parking lot, and headed home. Philip made a mental packing list and thought through the order of operations for getting to where Harriet planned to meet him, and Zak stayed quiet.

"Can I drive you to a train station or airport or something in the morning? Or turn around and do that right now?" Zak asked as they entered the house.

"No, that's all covered. I need get my things together, rest a bit, and then motor."

"Cool."

Philip used the front bench as a staging area, starting with kicking his sneakers off and retrieving his hikers from under it.

Most of what he'd take he kept always at the ready. Camera bag, a backpack with his preferred field clothes, the dorky but invaluable crossbody bag where he stashed his press ID and passport and funds. He moved light and preferred cheap, but this trip with blanket expenses paid, he figured he could forego making space for jerky and a can of peanuts and granola bars. In the morning he'd pack lunch and some extras.

"That's everything down here." Philip went upstairs to his room and efficiently loaded a small ditty bag with things like deodorant and a notebook and pen that would fit in the backpack.

Zak detoured to the bathroom and returned smelling minty fresh. He changed into sweatpants and stretched out on the bed while Philip packed.

"I've wondered when you'd run to chase a story and what that would be. And not like I'd stop you from heading into a war zone or some international intrigue, but this does seem a little safer."

"Compared to that? This is a cakewalk. Including the luxury of mid-range hotels that serve breakfast." Philip stood hands on hips and went over what he'd packed. "Probably the riskiest part will be the damn tiny prop planes. Nothing against the pilots, but those commuter runs aren't my favorite."

Philip went to the bathroom, used it, and then scrubbed his face and brushed his teeth. He carried back essential toiletries and zipped them into the ditty bag and then looked at Zak.

"Will you miss me?" Philip shouldn't ask and couldn't keep from asking.

"Yes." Zak held Philip's gaze and walked onto his palms to sit leaned on the headboard. His eyes darkened as Philip started to strip but he smiled. "Lots, loads, I'll pick up a hobby to distract me—all that. But it's your work and your talent, and I like seeing you with a story to chase down. I'm looking forward to reading it."

"I told you you're too well-adjusted. It's almost spooky."

"And I did say I'd miss you, and I really will need a distraction. Maybe I'll do the kitchen backsplash."

"If that's the case, I should have left sooner."

"I don't actually mind tile work. Or windows. I could weed the cracks between the patio stones too." Zak scraped his gaze from Philip's face to bare feet and back up, lingering on Philip's threadbare boxers and hands and chest, and then closed his eyes as if resisting. "Seriously, though, is there anything I can do while you're away or before you leave?"

"Fuck me," he rasped, unbidden and rife with sudden need, and pushed his boxers down. He didn't want Zak to resist. "Fuck me so I still feel you days from now."

Zak jerked upright like a livewire, seemed suspended for a moment, and then he groaned a deep exhale and started to move.

Philip held out a hand. "No, stay right there."

He stepped from his boxers and walked slowly to the bed, rubbing his fingertips over the line of his hip and then cupping his dick and stroking as it hardened, savored the power and pleasure of commanding

Zak's appreciation. He got their lube from the bedside table drawer and tossed it on the bed, then thought about where he'd have a condom.

They hadn't fucked yet. Zak clearly knew it was an option but hadn't brought it to their bed, much less playful or heated conversation, and Philip had no complaints. He might never have asked but the day had been so long and fraught and he was leaving in a few hours.

"Do you want easy clean-up or do you want it messy?"

Zak licked his teeth. "Messy." He reached for Philip in a scattershot touch, thumbing Philip's nipples and abs and the head of Philip's cock.

Philip knelt on the mattress and got Zak's sweats peeled off. He knee-walked to straddle Zak's lap.

"What do you need?" Zak asked and took hold of Philip's sides.

Philip hummed throatily. "You'll know when we get there."

He warmed lube in his palm and then thoroughly coated Zak's cock.

Zak sucked in a breath and closed his eyes and his grip tightened. When Philip let go, he opened his eyes and held Philip's gaze, and reached to feel Philip getting slick and open.

"Wish I could see it," he rasped.

"Next time," Philip laughed, and took Zak in hand and then worked Zak in by increments.

Zak kissed him, one hand on his cock, the other teasing and tugging his nipples. Philip shuddered and pressed down, and then Zak's hips punched, and Philip was fully seated.

"God you're big," he said roughly.

"Is it okay?" Zak's voice was strained, and he vibrated tautly under Philip.

"It's so good." Philip kissed the tension on Zak's brow. "Just been a while—but it's real good." He braced his hands on Zak's shoulders and arched his back and began to slowly rotate his hips. Then he lifted almost all the way off and then sank back down. "Big and good and perfect," he muttered and couldn't keep still.

Zak watched him fuck himself, on and on, rapt and attentive.

"Not—it's not enough," Zak finally gritted out when Philip refused to increase the pace. He nipped the soft strain of Philip's neck and wrapped an arm around Philip's waist, lifted and pushed with his legs, and then landed forward to Philip under him.

Philip consciously relaxed and opened his hips and bowed his back. Then he relaxed internally, breathed, and tightened again as he hitched his legs higher along Zak's ribs.

"Fuck." Zak's movements stuttered, and he freed his arm to plant his hand on the mattress. He planted his other hand on Philip's hip, heavy and anchoring and demanding.

Zak met Philip's gaze and made it hold and started pounding a hard, urgent rhythm. He changed his grip and the position of Philip's leg, fingers digging into Philip's thigh and then ass. Zak fucked Philip down the bed and didn't let up when Philip's shoulder and then arm flopped off the edge of the mattress.

Philip grabbed on to Zak's arm and tangled one hand in Zak's hair, moaned in ceaseless needy gasps, and his legs spasmed. The friction of their bodies and the constant pressure and sensation of Zak inside had him almost there—Philip grabbed his cock and came into the tightening sheath of his own fist from Zak fucking him.

Zak made urgent, incoherent noises as he grappled a firmer hold of Philip, nearly bent Philip in half, and then he growled when he found purchase and a steady pace.

Philip tingled and every nerve sparked as Zak kept going. He trailed his hands over the definition of Zak's abs and flanks and hovered a feather-light touch over Zak's nipples. Then he choked and then closed his eyes when Zak's force and speed increased, and then crested.

Zak stilled and came with a low shout. He stayed there, splayed a hand on Philip's middle and pressed one of Philip's hands to his heart, as they fought to breathe and slowly calmed.

Philip returned to awareness and Zak kissing and caressing his shoulders, the bumps of his spine, the jut of his hips. He smiled lazily and then sucked in a breath when Zak's slick fingers entered him, and he instinctively bowed his back and started rocking.

Zak stroked deeply and then fit his cock in the crease of Philip's ass, and then against Philip's hole, and then he stopped. Held there, and held there.

Philip rolled his hips. Pushed back but Zak evaded. Finally he tipped forward on his arm and reached back with his other hand, impatient and ready, and demanded Zak fill him again.

Zak did, hard and complete, and then stayed pressed to Philip and didn't move. Philip canted more and pushed his face into the mattress.

He let his legs ease apart, tightened their connection, rippled his insides again. Zak still didn't move. Philip whined, tilted his hips, and then started to release Zak and pull away.

Zak grabbed his middle and yanked him to the edge of the bed to stand on the floor and didn't make them wait any further. Philip worked his cock and groaned and then twisted to keep Zak hitting that perfect burning oversensitive molten spot. He came untethered and Zak lifted his loosened body higher, punched the air from him with hard and thorough ruts, and when Zak came, his grip made Philip moan and wince.

He hoped it'd bruise.

Philip crawled onto the bed and fell forward. Zak followed, pushed his top leg up and slid against him as close as possible, and then held them motionless.

"Okay?" he asked and kissed Zak's palm.

Zak's laughter was a low, pleased rumble. "Good, perfect." He pulled Philip even closer.

Philip lay there listening to Zak breathe, and then Zak drift asleep, until he had to admit he wouldn't be sleeping.

He slid off the foot of the bed and his legs almost gave out. After a dizzy minute, he grabbed his clothes and crept downstairs and had a quick wash in the bathroom. Then he grabbed a cushion and the box of long matches from the mantle and went out the front door. His mother's letters were in the bed of Zak's truck. He'd secreted them from the barn, tucked into his shoe, and before leaving the farm, stuffed them in the hold-all. He didn't want them or to read them, and he had to.

The waning moon lit the way as he invariably went to the overlook.

He set the cushion on one of the chairs and eased onto it and then stared into the dark. A breeze lifted and he savored its push—smelled good too—wet from the river and sweet from the garden. He caught the hoot of an owl and listened to a critter rustling in the trees. After a while he stirred and sorted the letters by postage date, braced, and wasn't at all prepared for how anticlimactic and mundane they were.

The letters were brief, vaguely coherent, clearly written in spurts both sober and not. Wanting to know about Philip's well-being was the first. Wanting money was the next two. The fourth and last a petty flounce, angry at Molly for not sharing enough, particularly money.

Philip hoped Molly hadn't sent any. He got the impression she didn't. It's part of why the letters ended as abruptly as they began. His mother had understood marks and opportunities, and when either had run dry.

Each letter did have a line or three of clarity that repeated how Philip was a good kid who deserved to do well in the world. He supposed that's why Molly held on to them. That and the simplicities of immediate indecision, stashing them away and forgetting. As good of reasons as any.

He reread them but there was nothing more to divine than her bald ask for money and lifelong indifference toward him. They were merely his mother, awful and banal and what he'd rightly left behind. Philip didn't find any reason to rethink the past or forgive her, her memory. But the shadow of her, the drive to escape and dread and anger were gone.

Even with the looming possibility of losing his house and the first real stability he'd known. He'd planned to burn them like some banishment or ritual but that seemed silly. Dramatic. Unnecessary.

Philip folded them into the matchbox and dropped that on the ground. He'd toss them in the recycling and that would be that.

"I was right that the chairs are perfect," Zak said from behind.

Philip wasn't startled. He'd wanted to sit there alone and wanted Zak to come find him. Zak nudged so he moved, and Zak got between him and the chair back. He tensed when Zak's handholds tightened but Zak only tucked him close with a blanket and then sat quietly.

"Did you at least rest?"

"Some. I can sleep on the flight."

Zak wanted to ask something, Philip could tell. What he did say Philip didn't expect.

"I've wondered this all along—I'm having a difficult time understanding why you tried to sell the house. It's obvious you belong here."

"My mom."

Zak took that in. "Did you inherit or have to deal with something she left behind?"

"Sort of the opposite, but yes." Philip debated how much Zak would want to hear, and wanted to tell everything. "I pried myself from her and her way of life when I was nearly fifteen and it's been on me to figure things out ever since."

"Was no one paying attention? Or around to help you?" Zak was incredulous, almost angry.

"No," Philip said baldly. "I could fend for myself by then and rattled around to safe enough places, got through high school and into college, and did everything I could to outrun her. I had plenty of money to buy this house, but after one too many things, no money to keep it."

It was an abrupt shift but Zak nodded. "After getting away and figuring things out, something she did still put you in peril."

Philip swallowed. "The house and running through my savings to fix it didn't scare me. I could work—there's always more work. Sling hash, dig ditches, win photography prizes, whatever. I also had grand plans to get a book written while I fixed the house—a working vacation from crisscrossing the world reporting. But the debt she caused, the price exacted, was bigger than that." He moved in a small jerk. "I got tracked down to be told she'd died in motel room. Overdose, diseases, both. Ostensibly to let me know, but it was as much so the state didn't have to bury her on their dime and as unclaimed."

"I'm so sorry."

"My only reaction was relief. When they first said her name, the things that spun through my mind were a thousand times worse than she was finally dead. Her dying was easy." Philip shifted. "That's something not a lot of people would understand."

"No, I get it. Believe me."

Philip did. "I went to Nevada and buried her, nothing fancy but nothing about that is cheap, and then when I got home, I couldn't write. I didn't want to take pictures. I didn't want to travel." He worked his jaw. "I could miter door trim and scrape paint and build cabinets, but my mind was blank. And editors think it's nice you have little hobbies like gardening, but it doesn't exactly do them any good if you garden instead of meeting deadlines. So I finally admitted I couldn't and didn't know when I would again, scraped together the book advance to get out of the contract, and paid it back."

"And so your choice became completely crushing debt or sell."

"Which, given, sell it was."

"That's… I don't even know. So hard and not what you deserved, and I'm sorry."

"I can't even claim she was complicated. She was just an uncomplicatedly not good person." Philip shrugged. "Not the only person like that roaming this world—I've met my share—she just happened to be my mother."

"I'm still sorry."

"Thank you." Philip hadn't taken sympathy from anyone, not even Tom. He let Zak guide his cheek to Zak's chest and hold him there for a long time.

He thought about Zak finding the house, getting here, who Zak had been.

"From everything I've read you were destined to go pro. Why didn't you?"

"My dad."

Philip didn't miss the echo. "I thought most dads want that for their kid."

"My dad couldn't wait. We had a list of teams we most wanted to draft me, he had a suit picked out for draft day, he was ready." Zak let out a shaky breath. "He was the best and my best friend. He loved football so I loved football, but as something to share, not him living frustrated ambitions through me or something."

"That's very sweet and sounds pretty great."

"Amazingly great." Zak flinched but started rubbing his cheek against Philip's hair and it seemed to calm him. "Then a pivotal game my senior year he dropped dead in the stands. A major heart attack and bam, gone. I learned about it on the sidelines."

"How awful, damn." Philip twisted up to see Zak. "I can't even imagine."

Zak blinked rapidly. "I don't remember the rest of that game. Everything became a blur, automatic. I do remember the next game—a home game—and everyone making a big deal when I took the field. It was well-intentioned and meant to be supportive, but I hated it."

"I can understand why."

"After that it's like I didn't know how to play, but I didn't know how to ask for a break either, so I stayed on automatic and gutted it out. But I did make a promise that if I got through the season and didn't lose my scholarship, I could walk away from the game and never explain myself. During our final game I got hit, hard, but nothing that should bench me permanently." Zak's hands drew into fists against Philip's ribs. "That hit… it was such a goddamn relief. I still could have gone pro, but I let it end my career. And let everyone assume the injury was worse than it was, and then the app exploded and gave me perfect cover to move on."

"Did you have anyone at all to talk to about it?"

"Not really. Coach had me in his office after the game when Dad died, but mostly wanted to hear I was all right and could keep playing. And my mom and siblings had their own grief." Muscles in Zak's arms twitched. "Looking back I'm like wow okay, definitely should have gone to counseling or something, but all I knew then was head down and push ahead. And it's not as if going from football to a unicorn tech success looks like a hardship from the outside."

"And after a while the going and going and going—it distances you so far from the hurt it seems like a solution, and also useless to go back." Philip covered Zak's hand. "Given *your* grief stole it from you, and made playing feel impossible, in some ways it's better that football was about you and your dad. With him gone there was still enough of your own identity remaining for you to move on."

Zak inhaled sharply at that. Philip's pragmatism grew into remorse the longer Zak stayed silent. The regret didn't make him think any differently—it's how he'd gotten through life—but he could have just been sympathetic.

"I never thought about it like that." Zak paused and then said reflectively, "Part of what I dreaded about playing was being forever defined by his death. I'd always be the star who didn't let it defeat me. So brave, so courageous, carrying on his memory. My retirement game was doomed to have some fucking montage of him run nonstop, and if I returned for old timer days or hall of fame anything, there it'd be."

"A ghost always with you."

"And one football owned, not me. This way he could rest—I could rest—but his memory is only mine." Zak exhaled. "Not to spite anyone, but—"

"Oh, spite them. Spite away. We can make a list and I'll spite them with you."

Zak huffed a strange laugh that turned into a low sob. Philip didn't try to do anything but let him, and to be there.

After several minutes Zak sniffed and freed an arm to mop up with his cuff. "I haven't cried about it in years."

"I've made you cry, how great. Another milestone reached."

"Look at us go." Zak squeezed Philip tightly and let out a long, long breath.

They subsided into comfortable quiet, but a question made Philip stir. "So how did you manage to be a football star and develop a winner app?"

"I had very little to do with it other than being suitemates with three decent guys. I couldn't afford off-campus housing and didn't care anyway, because to my thinking practice and games and travel made an apartment a waste. So I wound up the jock rooming with three computer geeks."

"And they made the app?"

"More or less. We ordered a lot of pizza that year, and one day I said splitting costs without needing cash should be possible, and their way of agreeing was to start coding." Zak's voice steadied as he talked and the upset soothed from his body. "They explained the whole process and even got me to do some grunt work, and have always given me partial credit for the idea, but they were looking ahead too. It was to their benefit to have a football star headed for the pros be the mouthpiece for a dinky money app."

"I'd guess when you sold it for tons, going pro or not no longer mattered."

"Pretty much. I was still known, and known as the likable guy, and I don't mind being the face of the company we formed out of that sale. Quite the senior year I had." Zak sighed a wry laugh. "These days hardly anyone equates me with football, and I don't mind that either."

"No one needs to suffer to make good things or good art, but I wouldn't be the reporter I am with all I've already done without growing up in neglect and determination to escape it. I know that, unequivocally." Philip found Zak's hand and laced their fingers together. "Real shit things can lead to so much better, especially if you're stubborn and lucky."

"That sounds right." Zak got Philip's other hand and pulled him close. "Good thing we're both in the ways we needed."

Nearly dawn found them still sitting there and Philip shivered. Being wrapped up in Zak wasn't cold but he needed to move—he also needed to get moving.

"So how about you shower, I make some breakfast, and we get you on your way?"

Chapter Eight

"I DON'T NEED to be babysat or anything, but check in when you can." Zak opened the front door for Philip. "I'm also actually interested to hear more about the story."

"Of course. And look at my, you know...." Philip waved a hand. "Whatever account Grady talked me into. I'm gonna do my best to actually use it."

"Imagine me eagerly awaiting updates as motivation." Zak handed Philip a thermos. "Coffee. Now go have an amazing trip and do great journalism things."

Philip initiated their kiss and then had to be the one to pull away. He gathered his stuff and Zak let him simply go, closing the front door behind him and not prolonging the goodbye. He appreciated it, and that Zak clearly recognized his demeanor had shifted into story mode and revving to work. But he could admit this was the hardest it'd ever been for him to leave chasing one.

He loaded the back seat and then dropped into the driver's seat and grimaced. Zak had certainly given what he'd asked. He let out a slow breath and shifted until the sensation was a low burn rather than sharpness. Philip put the car in gear and after that, traveling was automatic.

Car stashed at the tiny airport parking lot. Squash into a tin can and vibrate for hours. Land, find a bathroom, eat a convenience kiosk sandwich and bag of chips standing up, and then walk to the outer road ring and wait.

A nondescript but comfortable sedan pulled up to the curb, and then Harriet leaned over and opened the passenger door. She was as Philip remembered, petite and energetic, bob of dark hair, round lens glasses on a pleasant face and wearing a loose turquoise dress and trail sandals.

"Conyers, good to see you. Welcome to the Cape." She was rolling before Philip had the door closed again. "My hopeful itinerary is interviews in three places ahead of the storm, then if we need route inland to avoid it, and finish in the places the storm will have passed by the time we get there. I get the residents to tell me about their expectations and preparations for the storm, you get portraits as well as more editorial stuff, and then we jam it to the next place. See if a big storm and what it did to their beachy mansions changes any hearts and minds. Sort of an abstract before and after."

"Sounds fine by me. And this all includes?"

"Every last one is a fancy gated community. Here obviously, Rhode Island, and then Connecticut, Long Island, a spot in Jersey, and end in Delaware. Thematically we could hit the whole coast but that's obviously not feasible. We're in for a lot of driving."

"I'm good for it." Philip had buckled in and dug his notebook out. "What if nowhere gets hammered where you have interviews lined up?"

"Delaware is already getting outer bands, so we'll have something from that at least. Given the models, I'm betting the Cape and Connecticut will manage to skate unscathed. We won't waste a lot of time at either."

"All right. What are you needing from me, more specifically than you know I know how to take pictures?"

"Honestly? Half the reason I got these interviews was thanks to mentioning your priors that the would-be subjects felt very flattered by." Harriet had navigated them from the airport onto a main road; then she settled in to explain. "They think it's a sympathetic profile of their beachfront plight, that it's not climate change, that their crumbling real estate should still be worth millions. That kind of thing."

She jabbed her hand in the air as she spoke, and then pointed toward him. "I envisioned this as a months-long project. The editor who finally took it up wasn't in for hard-hitting or lengthy, then this out-of-season storm, and we've got a rush job. What I want is that you don't censor yourself, capture details and the reality of the situation, and flesh that out in your captions. The photos will be in one of those fancy parallel to the copy layouts, so you'll have the space."

"I can definitely manage that."

"Great. When you didn't respond right away, I was beside myself because I had to get moving, and I kind of already fudged to the interviewees you'd accepted." She laughed, no hard feelings. "So I'm doubly elated you were available at such short notice. It's going to be the difference in the piece I could get accepted and the one I can still tell."

"Happy to assist. I'm glad the strength of my past work helped get your foot in the door." Philip meant it.

Harriet turned the radio on and found a rock station. "We're not far from our first stop, so let me know if you want me to pull into a gas station or something ahead of that."

"I'm okay, unless you're hinting that I need to get cleaned up."

"You look like a suitably mussed, adventurous and hard-bitten photojournalist. Stick with it—you'll be just what they're hoping for."

Harriet hadn't been wrong, about that or the types of conversations she'd have. She was a skilled interviewer and coaxed more from everyone than they realized. Some among the families did believe in climate change and worried things were only accelerating, while in parallel fretting about how it could dare have affected them. A small-government near billionaire showed them his ongoing petition to get the state and then the feds to offshore dredge and bring the particulates onshore.

Philip played background, taking notes and photos of breakers and dying dunes and priceless bric-a-brac and some real Mid-Atlantic blue bloods. At the final mansion of the afternoon, the lady of the house asked for them to make time so he could get a family portrait of her, her husband, and their pack of Salukis, as she'd very much like one taken by a Pulitzer-winning photographer, and had every expectation they would.

Harriet offered pleasant excuses that they had to keep moving and Philip said flat-out no.

"I don't think anyone's snubbed her so bluntly in years," Harriet laughed as they got in the car.

"I made up for it by giving her my info and quoting a ridiculous rate if she ever wanted to schedule a portrait session in the future." Philip shrugged. "Never know, I could retire on this."

"Open up a whole new line of work. Always thinking on your feet, Conyers." Harriet grabbed an actual road atlas from behind her seat and made a quick check of the route. "Get moving, find dinner, evening interviews and keep on?"

"You're the boss." Philip jotted notes as Harriet inched past the security booth and waited to be let out again.

Well into Rhode Island she found a solid diner and Philip luxuriated in a patty melt and extra fries.

"How have you been? Besides awfully quiet for the last year and change." Harriet frowned mid-bite of her club sandwich. "Why have you been awfully quiet?"

"Busy with a book and I bought a house."

"Congrats on that. Whereabouts?"

"Upstate—closer to Buffalo than the city, actually."

"I hear it's pretty up there. And that it could get whipped by this storm, depending." She shifted her cup and plate to make space for her tablet. "I'm still just in my crummy little D.C. apartment. Do you like the house—I mean, owning it? And things are going mostly okay?"

"I do and they are, thanks. How about you and your crummy apartment?"

"It's perfect and I love it." Harriet laughed. "I'm barely there anyway. You know about that."

"All too well, and part of the reason for the house."

"I'm sure I'll get tired too. One day." She winked and then opened a weather app and started tapping around.

Philip ate her coleslaw and ordered coffee. Mentioning the book wasn't an overstatement or a lie. He'd worried his writing—the innate want for it as much as the drive—had atrophied or worse. But since last night he was seeing it again, angles and turns of phrase and snapshots in his mind's eye. Not only for Harriet's story but his own. He wasn't atrophied. He'd run too long on past-empty and was about to get incinerated by burnout.

He had bought the house in part because he wanted a little break. But then had only gone as hard fixing it so he could get back to work, and then couldn't figure out working after the dismal blow of his mother's death and what that'd cost him. Then Zak had barged in.

First as a wanted and heady distraction, but then shifting into a daily comfort, ease, actual rest, that he hadn't allowed himself in years. He'd have returned to a crummy apartment somewhere if not for all that, and because of far more than Zak's rent money. Months of nice groceries and regular sleep and good fucking worked wonders.

"Ready?"

Philip folded his napkin and tucked it under his plate, then stood.

"I'll pay," Harriet announced. "I get a nice per diem on this gig and we might as well use it. Meet you at the car?"

He made use of the bathroom and bought several candy bars at the counter. Clouds had started to clog the sky, so Philip leaned against the car and checked local and regional radar. It was apparently mayhem in southern Virginia. Looked like they'd cross paths with the storm in another full day and thread Harriet's needle.

The second round of interviews didn't offer much different, although Philip always liked being nosy professionally and seeing how other people lived. At one mansion on an enormous granite and marble terrace with sweeping views of the ocean, it occurred to him Zak could have this, and he knew with equal surety Zak wouldn't ever want it.

"Thinks paying taxes is a crime against him specifically, also thinks the county should sweep the beach of nesting shorebirds because he's convinced that's adding to the erosion." Harriet jammed her seat belt until it clicked and then gripped the steering wheel. "I'm glad not every last person we've talked to has been this level of entitled jerk, because I think I'd quit on the story right here."

"No, you wouldn't."

"No, I wouldn't." She started the car and drove the long causeway and then eased past the guard shack.

"Let me know if you need me to spell you," Philip offered as they put the coast behind them in favor of the interstate.

"Thanks. I'm good to get us to the hotel, but I might have you drive some tomorrow."

"Cool. I'm gonna sort today's work but if you start to zone out and need company, feel free to poke me."

"Roger roger that." Harriet snapped the radio on and put her foot down.

A few hours later they arrived. Harriet had them booked in a walk-in, let me help you to your room sir, hotel for the night. They got into the elevator, headed for different floors. Not the hardest day Philip had put in.

Harriet pushed Two. "Breakfast starts at six, our first interview is at nine, so I'm thinking leave around eight."

"I'll be right here right then," Philip promised and hit Five. The elevator smoothed to a stop and Harriet was stepping out. "Get some rest."

"Back atcha." She marched down the hall as the doors closed.

Philip slumped against the wall and cracked his neck. His room turned out to be a suite, large and plush and it seemed a waste for one night's sleep, but he made use of the steam shower and robe and snapped up every complimentary item he could find.

He climbed into bed and relaxed by increments and allowed tiredness in.

Miss you he wrote and took a picture of the empty expanse of the king bed. He looked from the photo to the bed and deleted everything. *Tried any macramé?*

Three dots appeared as Zak answered with gratifying speed. *Great suggestion, I'm already on the last crossword in the book. Going okay?*

Going good and it's a good gig. We knocked out what we needed today and on track for tomorrow.

Three dots appeared again, wiggled, and then disappeared. After a minute Zak wrote, *Keep a literal weather eye out and hope tomorrow goes as good as today.*

Philip didn't know what else to say without wanting to talk too much, so he answered, *And that's with an early start so I gotta snooze— talk to you soon.*

Zak replied with the sleeping emoji and *sleep tight.*

Philip slept crappy and woke easily. He ate alone in the breakfast room save for the attendants, took another steam shower just because he could, made sure everything was charged and in order and got to the lobby a bit before eight.

"Heya, champ. Ready to go?" Harriet wore a mustard-colored dupe of her dress from yesterday. "Breakfast is good here, right?"

"It really is." Philip got his stuff and they left their keycards on the desk on their way out. "I once stayed someplace where continental breakfast was white bread and jelly packets. No toaster. Of course I ate most of one loaf." He tossed what he wouldn't need in the trunk and got Harriet's bag in after. "And that's when you get food."

She patted her oversized purse. "And also why even on trips with expenses paid I load up on any breakfast granola bars and terrible bagels and fruit."

Philip tipped open his smaller bag to show off his bounty of the same.

"It's the only way." Harriet got in the car and them to the first of their mansions in short order.

Their day was much the same as yesterday, with longer distances to cover and worsening weather as they headed south. They left Long Island and skirted the city, and Philip drove past with the old familiar pang of it being home for so long.

"Miss it?"

"Some days. The museums, walking around all you need to find a meaningful story or great photo, takeout and delivery for twenty cuisines and not just pizza." Philip glanced in the rearview mirror at the skyline, changed even since he'd moved away, towering spires and thin spikes but the city still the same somehow. "But I wouldn't give up my place to go back just for moussaka and baklava delivered past midnight." He checked the rearview again and the framed capture of the city was gone—and didn't miss it at all.

"I think we got more from today than yesterday. Wider slate of opinions and personalities, no one blaming wildlife for taking out beaches."

"The Tulls were outright great. Planning an early retirement to the Upper Peninsula and bequeathing their property to land preservation efforts? Imagine if that was the majority instead. I got very flattering pictures of them."

Harriet snickered. "Another few hours to the hotel yet, but I'm good to hold dinner until we get there. How are you feeling?"

"Dinner later is fine. We can always break into our stale bagel stash."

"Let's book you a flight for as soon out tomorrow as possible. The weather is only going to get worse, and I want you headed home instead of stuck in Delaware with me." She paused. "That sounded more personal than I meant."

"No, I get it. And how bad?"

"It's stalled out over Delaware right now and will beat us to our Jersey stop—we'll be in it tonight. But I figure we can get you out from Baltimore or something and not chance everything being still grounded on the coast."

"Maybe I should stick around," Philip argued, as much with himself as Harriet. He probably should stay. Two years ago—less—it would have been no question. Going home sounded so good.

"Upstate you said?"

"Yep."

"Well, all the models have the storm hooking that way north of Philly instead of out and gone like before. There's going to be a story there for you—so no, let's just get you home."

Chapter Nine

Philip exerted all his will and travel wiles to make it home and not get stranded in a random city, bouncing through several airports and a connecting bus, and finally the last flight into the small regional airport to collect his car the following morning. He was no longer ahead of the storm but driving to meet it.

Harriet did get them pushed through the interviews and into Baltimore, where she planned to hunker at a friend's place and finish the story. As they'd navigated emptier and emptier roads and the backend of the storm, Philip had pared his files to what he considered were the best photos and handed her some data sticks. During his flights, he wrote captions for her to choose from, sent as he could manage from packed waiting areas at various airport connections.

His final look and photo was a massive wave about to swallow a buckling mansion, perched on a natural jut into the ocean, several properties down the beach from where they stood. That location had probably been every neighbor's envy.

Then they'd been hustled along by security and next a sheriff, slaloming debris and standing water and stalled cars, until Harriet found a cleared road and got them out.

He was doing much the same but was almost there. The rain had paused and the sky was inky-green and the air eerily calm. He knew none of that was a good sign.

Philip's heart jumped when he turned into the driveway. Even after all the shitty hours awake and traveling and in the sights of the coming storm, he almost couldn't stop grinning at the sight of the house and Zak's truck out front. He was impatient to get inside and shut the door on the world.

He parked and then sat. He tempered his emotions, made his pulse slow, calmed his weirdly giddy mind. Then he gathered his bags and squared his shoulders and walked sedately to the house.

Philip lowered his stuff onto the bench and had to wait for his eyes to adjust. Aside from a strange flickering light, the house was dim, almost dark. He crept into the living room and everything slammed to a halt.

Zak napped on the couch, laptop open to an endlessly looping weather radar map, one arm slung to the side and the other curled around Maddie, snug and asleep under the span of his hand.

Philip's heart skipped three beats and then sped past what he could control.

Oh no. Oh fuck no.

He stared at them, comfy and trusting and totally oblivious, and then spun on his heel. Thick coppery air swamped him as he kept walking, almost running, until he was in the middle of the road. Then he bent forward with his hands on his knees and squeezed his eyes closed.

Philip missed home so sharply and wanted to grin and shout because Zak was there. Because Zak being there meant it was home. Because he'd fallen head over heels completely besotted in love with Zak.

Huge, soaking raindrops began to drum down but Philip didn't move.

He'd been in love with Zak for a long time. Being wrung-out and worried and racing to get back was finally enough to two-by-four him in the face to admitting it. That and Zak completely zonked and cozy with Maddie so secure on Zak's chest, in the house, did something to him.

Did he want a freaking baby? That he wasn't sure about, but he did want Zak to keep him in nice groceries and regular sleep and good fucking. He wanted Zak to keep him—to keep Zak.

Philip straightened and scrubbed his face with his hands. He tugged his hood up and laughed at his obstinate foolishness, and because he was in love. There wasn't enough road to keep going and outrun that, so he turned back around and trudged to the house.

"I think he's home, wait I hear him," Zak's voice drifted from upstairs.

Philip took the stairs two at a time and met Zak on the landing. Zak was awake, adorably mussed and pacing. He handed Philip his phone.

"Hello?"

"Philip, bud, geeze it's good you made it." Tom talked over the noise of hammering rain. "We tried to get Kelly's dad to the commuter train but there's just been roadblocks and being told to turn around. It's taken us most of the day to drive almost nowhere, but we're finally almost home and on our way to get Maddie."

"Actually, meet me somewhere. Then you don't have as far to go."

"Are you sure? Things will deteriorate fast but we're still just ahead of it."

"I'm going anyway, so if the weather isn't complete shit yet and it's safe, I'll bring her to you."

Tom said something to Kelly and she answered but Philip couldn't make it out.

"Okay, sounds good. It's gotta be in like twenty, though, or you're keeping her overnight at least—I think Zak has an extra bottle. How about the old church at the split?"

"Done. See you soon." Philip set Zak's phone down, slithered from his coat and pried off his boots, and ran upstairs. "Can you get her ready?" he called as he changed into dry clothes, grabbed a pair of high-wick socks, and clomped downstairs again.

Zak had Maddie in her carrier and was arranging raingear to put on.

"No, I'll just go." Philip sat on a stair and shoved into the socks and his boots.

He stamped his feet to get his pant cuffs to drop and then he shifted gears to prepare for going into an uncertain, and likely unstable, situation. The drive to meet Tom would be short but he didn't intend to stop there or simply turn around and come home, and he'd need gear and supplies to be ready for that.

Philip riffled through his camera bag and backpack, exchanging batteries and choosing lenses, and zipped his wallet into a compartment. He dug an older coat from the closet along with a poncho, and quickly decided on a pocketknife, an emergency kit, and an extra flashlight. Since he was indecisive about food, he went with bringing food, upending his backpack onto a chair as he headed into the kitchen. He packed snacks and water and everything else standing at the bench and then turned to get Maddie.

Zak had dressed in the raingear and her carrier still in hand.

"I said—"

"We'll both go. What if there's something in the road or one of us has to walk ahead or something? And I assume you want to see what's happening—see if there's a story—so when we get to town I can help. You getting that story or just whoever else needs it."

Philip didn't have the luxury of arguing and he didn't want to either. "Then it makes the most sense to take your truck."

Zak flashed his keys, already in hand. "That's what I thought."

Philip opened the front door into the storm and paused, popped onto his toes so he could kiss Zak, and then bent into the rain.

Getting to the old church wasn't harrowing but also not a normal drive. Maddie slept blissfully through blinding lightning and rattling thunder and Philip getting someone's errant garbage bins out of the road. He was glad to see Tom's car parked there and waiting.

Zak pulled alongside as close as possible, and Kelly jumped out to transfer the baby. They'd chanced into a break in the bands of rain, so things were weirdly calm again. Philip wrapped his grip on the door after Tom rolled the window down and pushed it back shut.

"Franklin, good to see you, considering," he said over Tom's shoulder to Kelly's dad.

"Stay safe taking your damn fool pictures," Franklin answered and then turned to get Maddie buckled in.

Philip kept his hold on the door when Tom pushed.

"Hey, I can help. You guys don't need to be out in this by yourselves."

"And you don't need to be out here at all. It's bad enough we're doing this." Philip swept a hand upward and shook his head. "You're not even a volunteer fireman, Tom—and you're a father now. Go home. Everyone will need you more in the coming months."

"Listen to your best friend, sweetie." Kelly slammed her door and leaned down to see Philip. "Damn fool pictures sure, but don't do anything wildly risky."

"Got it, medium risky or less." Philip thumped the roof. "Now get on, we'll talk soon."

Tom grumbled but understood it was right. He rolled up the window, waved and tipped a finger at Zak, and then eased away.

They wasted no time getting in the truck and to town before the rain picked up again. Zak parked on Main Street and Philip came around the hood, deciding where to start.

"Coach!" someone yelled.

Zak looked at Philip and he nodded and followed Zak's trot across the street to the sheltered entryway of the hardware store. The core of the defense team were packed in there, dressed in raincoats and work boots or hikers.

"What are you guys doing here?" Zak asked.

"We were all messaging about the storm and decided we had to help," Braden said for them.

"We're… planning what to do first," Liam offered.

The boys had a brave face but were clearly uneasy and wanted guidance. Zak hesitated. Philip had lived this before.

"Did the mayor or anyone official communicate about a shelter, or a reunion and recovery center?" he asked.

Braden spoke up again. "Yep, the old high school gymnasium."

"Great, you guys head there. They'll need whatever help they can get—setting up sleep spaces, organizing the influx of donations, keeping kids entertained, that kind of thing. You all can handle that easy," Philip said with level confidence so they'd think so too.

"My house is on the way. We can stop and get old blankets and stuff."

Philip remembered that kid as Jerome.

"If we go out of town first, we can go to my place too," Liam added.

The other boys started to chatter about who could get to whose house and Philip cut them off.

"No, don't. You made it into town all right, but who knows how the conditions have changed since then? Go to Jerome's, and while you're there, text all of your parents where you're going to be, and then when you get to the gymnasium, find who's in charge and get to work."

Grady nodded. "We'll tell them you sent us."

"At least tell them Coach did," Philip joked and got a ripple of laughter. "And stay put until at least morning. Driving around in this is dangerous, even for people with equipment and experience."

"Yes, sir," Grady answered for them.

The energy of the group changed, buoyed and energized, and the boys' restlessness shifted from uncertainty to purpose.

Philip crossed his arms. "Text Coach in the morning too and let him know how you're doing."

"Can do." Braden held a hand out and got a fist-bump from Zak, and then waited for one from Philip.

"I've got my camera too," Grady told him. "I'll get some good shots at the gym."

"I know you will." Philip patted Grady's shoulder.

Then the boys chorused goodbyes and ran in a huddle across the street, crammed into two pickups, went a block, and turned.

Zak watched them go. "That was a good call."

"There really will be plenty for them to do, but mostly I'm glad none will get themselves killed." Philip considered his options. "I want to go to the police station. I vaguely know the chief, and he knows that I'm a 'bigshot' reporter who moved to town."

"Hopefully that will be easy enough. It's just down the street." Zak bore them to his truck and Philip stayed silent as he drove.

Philip huddled into his coat and pushed into the building, Zak on his heels. The rain had increased, as had the wind.

He wasn't surprised to find a hive of activity and no one at the desk. He also didn't wait for permission to wade into the bullpen and past to a briefing room full of officers, town employees, the fire crew, and EMTs. But he went no farther than standing at the back wall.

"Gentleman," the chief said, his gaze flickering with recognition. "I was just getting into the unique conditions threatening us, so get your notepad out," he said to Philip.

Philip stopped readying his camera to hold up a pen. He snapped a few phone pictures of the scene, the chief, Zak listening.

"Good." The chief stood in front of a large monitor that looped the radar over a map of the area. "Our biggest concern is rain—this storm is now a rain event. Wind is still a factor, but we're going to get hammered by precip." He pointed at a specific spot on the map. "Upriver ten miles is a confluence joining the Klikli River we straddle. The valley narrows precipitously at this point and doesn't widen again until about one mile north of town. That means all of this—" He circled his hand over the narrowed section. "—backs water up and adds force so it becomes a flume that will overrun us."

"So we're talking a flood?" someone asked.

"Without a doubt and if the predictions hold, a very bad one."

Murmurings grew to partitioned conversations and questions all at once. Philip stashed his camera and nudged Zak, and waved at the chief as they shuffled out.

"Now what?" Zak asked as they headed to the door.

"Walk around, get some pictures, try not to get washed away, the usual." He paused in the vestibule and got his poncho out and on over his gear and then posted the pictures he'd taken inside. "Do you want to stay in the truck? Or here?"

"I'm not ashamed to say I'm seriously considering it."

"How about this—head to the old high school. The boys will be glad to see you, and I'll meet you there."

Zak frowned. "And if hours and hours go by?"

"Stay put and worry about me in the morning."

"I'll worry about you regardless, but I promise I won't barge into this mess to come looking."

"Fair enough." Philip fitted a cap on and tightened his hood around it. "I'll be fine."

"You'd better."

They didn't make it more than that, parted ways when they got to Zak's truck, and went opposite directions. Philip ventured everywhere he dared, to the low side of town with its hasty piles of sandbags, crossing the river on bridges that shook from the force of the water, coaxing a ride along from an ambulance that happened by.

Tree branches cracked and it was difficult to discern hearing anything beyond the white noise of the unending rain and rushing water. When the power went out, he lost the contrast of artificial light trying to peer through the storm, and his pictures became slurry and dark. He probably would keep on going through the night if Zak weren't waiting for him, at the police station if nothing else, but Zak did wait and Philip didn't mind.

Zak's gaze watchful on the door into the gym and evident relief when he appeared made him glad he didn't stay out longer. As always he took pictures, and might even have caught Zak's expression.

"Think we should spend the night?" he asked as Zak met him by the door.

"Maybe not? Maybe. If we lived across the river no way, but we're climbing out of the valley. A deputy was by twenty minutes ago to help get the generators going, and he said there are roads still clear. The wind's really died down, so if we can avoid runoff and flooding, we're good."

Philip weighed the options. "I'm willing to chance it, and willing to turn right around to bunk here if there's trouble."

"Agreed." Zak touched Philip's arm. "I'm gonna tell the boys and all you're okay, and that we're going to try for home."

Conditions had gotten worse but not life-threatening. Zak kept to the crown of the main roads and Philip's shoulders lowered a few inches when they turned into the driveway. The truck headlights swept across the house and Zak stomped on the brake.

"Shit." Zak threw the truck into Park.

Philip was out and stepping into the harsh beams and pelting rain before he could even think to gape at what had happened. The ancient, enormous oak with decaying limbs and a high up cavity nest he loved and worried about had snapped—and taken the front corner of the house with it.

After moving in he'd consulted with an arborist, who'd advised it'd be fine, could be fine but for a once-in-a-century storm, and what were the odds of that before it was properly dealt with? He wanted to weep. He could rage. He would pull the entire goddamn house down with his bare hands.

Philip heard Zak talking but couldn't listen. Six months rent from Zak was the mortgage and expenses, not mortgage and expenses and rebuilding. Even six months more would barely make a dent in that. He stared at the house and forced every reaction to subside and then drain from him as if flowing with the rain.

Anger and shock had to be short-lived. Neither would do him any good. Keeping your wits about you is what kept you alive and going, not wasting energy on freaking the fuck out.

"No, don't," he said as Zak cautiously approached the front door. "Nighttime's the most dangerous to go into anywhere unstable. There's nothing immediate that can be done about it anyway." He went to his car and reached under the rear bumper, whapped his hand around until it grazed a small plastic box, and pried that loose.

Zak came over to him. "What's up?"

"Head to the farm and crash. There's room even with Kelly's parents. And I can't think there's any motel reliably open at this point." In the past Philip would have slept in his car and bothered no one, but he didn't want to sleep in his car and Tom would say him doing so was the imposition, not showing up in the final throes of a monster storm. He slid the lid off the magnetic box and tipped a spare key into his hand. "Let's drive separately because who knows what we'll need to do in the morning."

"Sure, makes sense. The nearest motel with vacancy or service is probably farther than I'm up to finding anyway." Zak sensed his mood, fit a hand to his neck, and gave him a quick kiss but then backed away. "I'll follow."

Philip flipped on the fog lights and drove slowly. He had to reverse out of a secondary road and go out of their way when he realized the sheen he saw was a torrent of water and not wet pavement, but there were no other hazards. The farmhouse made a bright, reassuring beacon, and Philip drove the long driveway and then right back down it to park. Zak pulled in behind him, and they walked to the house where he let them in.

He stripped to his soaked cargos and damp T-shirt and arrayed his coat and gear on kitchen chairs and doorknobs as Zak did the same.

"Shit, you two look like drowned rats." Tom strode into the kitchen, threw together a pot of coffee and flipped the maker on, and then crossed past Philip to the laundry room. "Toss whatever's washable in. I'll be right back."

Philip dropped his outer layers in the washer and peeled his pants off, grimacing as they clung with weird suction and how cold they'd gotten. An enormous towel landed on and slithered down his back as he worked on his socks.

"Philip, go jump into our shower. Zak, take the bathroom next to the nursery, and meet me in the kitchen in twenty." Tom had dry clothes that he handed to them as they walked past and to their assigned showers.

After being drenched for hours, a shower shouldn't be so good. Enveloping heat and getting clean was in another dimension from rain and flood yuck. Philip dressed in Tom's old sweats and thermal shirt and appreciated most the dry socks, and returned to the kitchen in under fifteen. He got his phone from the table and then just stood there.

Tom pushed him into a bar stool and then shoved a mug of coffee under his chin and an empty plate to his elbow. "Leftover extravaganza, help yourself."

He went with mac and cheese and mashed potatoes and several rolls, discovered as he ate that he was famished, and not much had ever tasted so good. Zak joined him, sat purposefully close so their thighs and arms touched, and polished off the mac and cheese and made inroads on some meatloaf.

"Everyone okay?" Tom asked after their eating had slowed down.

"So much better, thanks." Philip accepted a refill of coffee and sat back in the chair. "Depending on what's available or not, we might need to come back tomorrow to sleep. And the tomorrow after that." He glanced at the microwave and hadn't realized it was so late—it was tomorrow already.

"Of course. Is your power out?"

"The house is out." Philip sliced his hand through the air. "The storm took a tree and the tree took the house. At the least some of the roof and the northwest front façade is gone."

"Goddamn, I'm so sorry. And I was annoyed the middle paddock flooded."

"Given it's the goat's favorite and blocks access to the south paddock, that is annoying." Philip tapped his mug. "And thanks. I'm… trying not to doomsday it. And very glad to just show up and get fed and have somewhere to be in the meantime."

"Hey, man, as long as you need." Tom cleared their dishes and replaced the hot food with a pan of brownies. He didn't press for details, in part because it was clear none could be known yet.

Zak drew Philip's hand into his lap and opened Philip's palm over his thigh and covered it, and then grabbed a brownie.

Tom worked two brownies from the pan. He leaned against the counter. "Your posts from tonight were incredible, as in the almost-defies-belief way. We watched coverage on TV all night, and it was reassuring to know you hadn't been swept away or something."

Philip poked at his phone to check the posts and boggled at the likes and comments and shares. He hadn't thought of them a moment past capturing the images, the brief captions, and moving on. Littering the comments were reporters who wanted to use his stuff—with credit, they promised, but he could really use some coin instead—and it didn't take long to find his pictures stolen and posted on other people's feeds.

"Fuck," he muttered, too weary to be angry but definitely up to feeling bitter about it.

"What?" Zak's attention was immediate.

He just spun his phone on the counter so Zak could see and ate a brownie.

"The people willing to give you credit don't offer money, and the people who want money don't offer credit." Zak nudged the phone back to Philip. "A fundamental law of being online."

"People lifting your stuff again?" Tom had heard his share of Philip's rants on the subject.

"Invariably. See, this is why I don't post. Or didn't." Philip rolled his shoulders and then an impressively huge yawn overtook him.

"You guys hit the sack. We'll tackle things fresh in the morning."

Philip finished a brief email he chanced sending to his editor about the book first. Said in brief he'd cleared the complications and let's talk. With half his house knocked in, he needed that advance, but it was more than that. In the past weeks, words had returned to him. The rest had done him good. But mentoring Grady, the story with Harriet, and tonight especially was a shot of adrenaline that jolted back his creativity and drive. There was something very clarifying about being in the teeth of a storm and snapping into action.

Then he slid to his feet, patted Tom's arm as he went past, and trudged upstairs.

He crawled to the wall side of the bed and curled up under a pile of quilts, a mix of nervy and wrung out, mind whirling with stories and images and what to do about his house. It'd take him a while to wind down and fall asleep—if he even did.

The old double bed groaned under Zak's weight and jostled Philip.

Zak lay down, rolled over, and pulled Philip into his arms. "I can hear the buzz of your brain bees," he whispered. "Smart and determined as you are, you can't fix the roof with your mind. And you're who said it can't get done tonight."

"No, but I can fixate on multiple scenarios and their order of operations until I have to get up and start dealing with it in the morning."

"That does sound wonderfully excruciating." Zak nestled Philip's hips farther back into his and tilted enough so Philip took, and felt, his weight. "Or you could humor me and listen to the app idea I finally had."

Philip hummed, not quite *I guess* and not really *go on*.

Zak simply kept talking. "All these months in the ideal setting for quiet reflection and creativity, and of course it's a disaster that inspires me. Well, a combo of disaster and your photos, and those getting immediately scraped."

Philip tried to connect those dots but couldn't quite.

"I've used these map apps for backcountry hiking or getting around with limited data that run on GPS. That's a great framework for my idea—implement GPS mapping to help during and recovery from disasters."

Zak took hold of Philip's hand and stretched their arms across the bed, and then began rhythmically stroking Philip's arm up and down, up and down.

"Users get the app, download the map of their region, and can then get GPS-enabled updates pinged to them. Bridges out, funnel touchdowns sighted, load in pictures to populate on the map showing damage or things in need of rescue. Crowdsourcing sure, but available to first responders and municipalities as well. But—and this is where your pictures come in—encrypt them so they can't be scraped and profited from. See what I mean?"

Philip wanted to say kind of, not really, and managed an indistinct mutter.

"Exactly." Zak kissed behind his ear. "Ideally we'd swing it as a freebie app but if not, ad buys should be unobtrusive, maybe something like getting priority location spotting or placement on the everyday, muted during actual emergency events, and then easily dismissible billboards in the immediate aftermath. We'd have to filter hard for predatory and hack services, though. I also imagine adding a notation function so people can communicate without needing data…."

The next Philip was aware, Zak had fallen asleep, they'd separated to lie facing each other, and the incipient glow of dawn showed through the windows. He smiled at Zak, worn-out and snoring lightly, handsome and a mess from last night, there. Present, with him, for him.

Philip kissed his fingertips and pressed them to Zak's forehead, flopped onto his back, and then quick as that was fully awake and itching to move.

He gracelessly made it out of bed along the wall and found Tom in the kitchen, walking Maddie in slow passes around the house. Tom turned and managed to be comically startled without making a sound. He rounded his eyes hugely and came over to Philip.

"Morning," Philip said quietly.

"Damn, you're up early. She got fussy about an hour ago, so we've been doing this ever since." Tom checked Maddie and smiled. "She's finally out again, but I think we'll just walk some more. It's nice. Kind of meditative."

Philip nodded and got changed in the laundry room, snagged some reusable bottles from a shelf, and then started making a PBJ because that was fast and filling.

"Use some of Kelly's caffeinated flavored stuff," Tom said as he passed an upper cabinet and gave it a tap. "There's like a billion to choose from."

He went with three bottles of fruit punch and slapped together a second sandwich. Tom went with him to the front door, where he stuffed his shoes mostly on and borrowed one of Tom's big rain slickers as his gear had barely dried.

"I've gotta go see the aftermath and it won't keep." He patted his camera bag. "In town and my house."

"Right, that makes sense. Your pictures from last night are already all over."

"Ah well." It was a win and a lose at once. Philip remembered Zak putting him to sleep talking about the app and he crossed back to the kitchen and a side countertop, tugged open a drawer, and wrote a quick note. "Give this to Zak when he gets up?"

"Can do, bud."

Philip kissed Maddie's forehead and then snagged his car keys from a hook by the front door.

Tom followed him onto the porch. "The house can be fixed, you know—we'll get it figured out."

Thinking about the damage made his insides squirm and his defenses want to slam in place, but he pushed that aside. "I know."

"Be safe," Tom whisper-shouted as Philip crossed the crowded driveway.

Philip saluted, walked past the knot of cars to where he'd parked, and then tediously picked his way to town. The river ran fast and dangerous, branches and boulders and hunks of houses churning in dizzying whitecaps. Philip parked in the middle of the road more than once to get pictures of debris lines and clear obstacles and be certain huge puddles wouldn't swamp the car.

Green leaves stripped from trees covered signs and fences and the high ground. Brown muck clung to houses and tree trunks and saturated wherever it had reached. A bright blue sky filled with picturesque clouds jarred against the dismal scenes on the ground.

He stopped and talked to a family without power who'd decided to spend their day doing whatever they could instead of waiting around. He'd stayed with them a bit, taking pictures, getting their thoughts, and then assisting their chainsaw and cutter jaws and dragging felled trees from the road.

Philip stashed the car at the mechanic he used, situated about a quarter mile from town and made the rest of the way on foot. As he crossed the invisible boundary from country road to outskirts neighborhood, he shifted into his keenly alert mode of always listen, make little sound, and talk less.

Familiar landmarks were damaged or moved or outright gone. The center of the bridge he'd stood on yesterday was no more, so he carefully stepped to the first footing and got sweeping shots of the aftermath, high side of town mostly standing, low side of town on the opposite shore partially submerged in what the river had left behind.

The river thundered, mixing with the aggressive whine of more chainsaws and equipment and punctuated by bullhorn and siren blips. Philip passed homes, and then shops, the green, and then was in the square. Peering in the law office window showed a line of muck that'd lapped in past the threshold, but solid old stone construction and the good fortune of being at the limit of the river's reach had spared the line of buildings.

He texted pictures to Tom and agreed with Tom's relief at the lack of damage.

An emergency command center bustled in the town hall and Philip lurked in the corners, listened in, and then talked to the fire chief and a rescue group from downstate. He got a photo of the map filled with color-coded pushpins that represented cleared neighborhoods, areas of concern, and places no one had gotten to yet. The whole floor went quiet when the latest weather forecast squawked on someone's radio, and he took pictures of people hearing the tail end of the storm that could bring more rain had broken up and might add drizzle to their list of headaches in the coming days, but nothing else.

Other media circled and he recognized a prominent anchor from a weather news network, but the townsfolk preferred him.

He hitched a ride with a dump truck that got a different rescue group across the river, and then in their boat as they went door-to-door checking houses. He stayed with that for a while and didn't mind the monotony or lack of excitement but when they met a small flotilla of boats headed to high ground, he said his thanks and returned to the town square.

Everyone he talked to had a similar story and wore shock he'd seen before. Philip understood from past experience that cleaning up and rebuilding would take longer than anyone imagined, recovery was possible, and some things would never come back. He also knew people would rebuild what they shouldn't and lessons wouldn't be learned and losses from the next freak storm could dwarf this. But realistic as he was, he hoped that didn't happen for a long time.

He could keep nosing around but he knew the story was played out for the day. The routine he'd seen would repeat tomorrow and tomorrow, and then morph into protracted efforts and the slog of putting things to rights. Philip wrote a brief summary of who he'd met and what he'd seen and started to walk back to the car.

"Eric?" Philip answered his phone, surprised it'd rang and surprised it was his would-be book editor.

"That storm cut quite a swath, but it looks like an apocalypse up there—are you okay?"

Philip considered it. "I am. I got lucky."

"That's something at least. I'm sure you're not in the mood for chatting so I'll cut to the chase that no can do on the book, at least for now."

"Thanks for letting me know," *what could have been an email* Philip added with grim humor.

"I called because this won't wait. What I can offer instead is if you keep posting pictures and stories of what folk are going through, and we'll use them to launch this newsletter-online magazine thing we've wanted to get started."

"I can do that." He'd intended to continue posting and writing about the storm's aftermath, so his ready answer was simple.

"Super. Stay with your approach of the personal meeting climate change angles. It's a strong mix and speaks to the more highbrow tone we want to curate. And, in all crassness, capitalize on keeping Zak Springer centered. His presence is clearly part of why this particular storm in your particular small town has gone viral. Okay?"

"I can do all that too."

"And this work is exclusive to us. Yes, keep posting, but the longer form stuff will be for the newsletter."

Philip thought that over. "I'm good with that if given sufficient compensation."

"Glad to hear it. Also glad to get to you ahead of anyone else." Eric finally took a breath. "All right, we'll draft a contract and terms and get that to you digitally ASAP and cc your lawyer. And with permission, I'll work up some shorts based on what you've already shared. No major changes and nothing editorial, just to get it to our mailing list while it's hot."

"Sure, that's fine. I know you can tease the best stuff from my raw work."

"That is my job." Eric's relief and enthusiasm to get started was evident. "I'll let you go but email with any questions and, between us, I think that book could still happen if this newsletter does as well as we project, given the response to your storm stories so far. That'll be some good momentum for it in a year or so."

"I'm ready to write it," Philip said, and meant it.

"Fantastic. M'k, all right." Eric wound down, and then added sincerely, "Take care, Philip."

"Will do. Thanks, Eric." Philip hung up and stared at the phone.

Contract for steady work, renewed life on the book he wanted to write—what had Zak said—only took a disaster.

"Speaking of," he muttered as an avalanche of texts from Zak arrived before he'd pocketed his phone.

Sorry to text this but it can't wait (and sorry if I overstepped) but I asked around and found a reputable group from North Carolina who specialize in old houses and slate roofs, including structural. They're not affected by the storm and can be here tomorrow, start work as soon as the tree's cleared. There's plenty more slate from the old quarry at Braden's to match the path.

Or we can figure something else out. You can. I'll cosign a loan or whatever is best for you.

Let me know.

Philip knew this was the only way for the house to get fixed correctly and with any speed, and given the damn roof was gone, urgent speed was required.

Do it. Philip answered. *Thank you.*

Zak shot back a thumbs-up and a heart and went quiet again.

He'd gotten as far as the green, which was busy and bustling since he'd last seen it churned up and quiet. Grilling and food smells wafted to him, and his stomach rumbled. A line of people waited to head along a row of tables; Philip recognized some EMTs he'd talked to earlier and then he spotted Barb.

"How'd you come through?" he asked and took over spooning fruit salad into cups for her.

"Philip, good to see you. We've been following your posts all day, so I can say not as bad as some." Barb tugged her apron up and wiped clammy rain moisture and sweat from her face. "Lost everything on the terrace, from the big tables down to the fairy lights. And the old shed in the parking lot. But the restaurant's fine, so I'll be fine. No power, though, and I'd just had a load of food in. No reason to let it go to waste, so here we are."

"I'm glad to hear it, including that I'm in dire need of a very late lunch." Philip scooted cups around and filled gaps on the table. "Is it okay if I hang out for a bit and talk with people about how they're doing?"

"So long as you keep slinging hash? Stay as long as you like." Barb nodded once and then held up a finger, stepped down the line, and returned with two sausage biscuits wrapped in a napkin. "Get those in you and after you're done with your reporting, have your fill."

"I'll talk to you last," he promised, and then gobbled the biscuits between fruit cups and then macaroni salad duty.

He stayed on that for a few hours, chatting but mostly listening, and then he passed the spoon to someone else. He bolted down a plateful of food, got some good pictures, and then started walking for the car again, glad for the huge takeaway cup of coffee that warmed his hands.

Philip yawned when he got into his car as fatigue at last caught up with him. He reversed and headed home, and kept an eye out for the family doing clean-up but didn't see anyone else on the road. He parked at the end of the driveway and preemptively walked it, moved some hefty branches and uncounted sticks, and then parked in front of the house.

The tree that'd crashed his house wasn't the enormous oak as he'd thought. It had fallen, but it was a smaller tree that had clearly taken its brunt and diverted the fall. Philip went into the woods and stared down the length of the great old tree lying parallel to the driveway, its crown taller than him by several feet, the roots like a ripped open shell rending a crater in the earth.

"Sorry, old fellow," Philip said and patted the trunk.

He'd leave it to become bird and bug and animal homes, to nourish the ground, to make way for saplings that would race to fill the canopy. He'd miss its stately presence, flushed orange in autumn, whispering its dried brown leaves in winter, the brightest green in spring, pattering acorns while creaking in the wind. But at least left there to decompose, it would remain for decades more, keep him company a different way, be allowed the dignity of finishing its full lifecycle.

Philip patted the trunk again and then went to stand in front of the house. Maybe not the enormous oak that'd fallen, and still plenty of damage done, but not the catastrophic ruin he'd feared. His old, quirky, and sturdily built house had presented its share of headaches, but those same qualities absorbed the impact of the tree with a bruise instead of a full break.

A big, ugly, cost-a-fortune bruise. But it could have been so much worse.

The front door opened like nothing had happened. Sunlight shafted into the foyer and the stairs were a wet mess covered in leaves and storm debris. He climbed slowly, and at the top turned to the front and looked into sky. The temptation to go and peer out the gash ripped in the house was great, but he stayed put. Obvious losses were the roof, the weird eaves attic space over the kitchen, the round leaded window he'd installed in the weird eaves attic space, and part of the guest bedroom.

Philip unplugged his laptop and then turned it on. It booted up fine. His framed photographs were waterlogged but could be reprinted—or left as a loss and the opportunity to choose something new. Shut the door on his bedroom and everything could be forgotten.

"Everything looks better in the morning, unless rent's due," he said, one of the few things his mother said he kept with him as right.

He left his bedroom and closed the door and walked down the hall as far as he dared. The interior could be dealt with in time, but he knew nothing about mitigating a giant hole in the roof. Should he get a tarp—did they make tarps that big?

His phone rang and Philip dug it from a pocket, expecting Zak or Tom, maybe Eric again, but it was an unknown number.

"Hello?"

"Philip, hi. Zak passed along your number—this is Henry by the way—I hear you have a big tree problem."

"Big in myriad ways. I'm staring at it now, point of fact."

"Man, that's rough. And I'm sorry to talk so soon because of it and not shop stuff. But listen, we're absolutely swamped helping with emergency work and I expect that to go into the night, but we can be at your place in the morning."

"To do what?"

"Oh sorry, I figured Zak or Tom would have gotten to you first. My family own and operate an old-school sawmill. My dad added the tree surgery stuff years ago, and then I got us into woodworking. Anyway— to deal with the tree. We'll bring the bucket truck and a mill, assess, and start breaking her down. If there's usable lumber out of anything, that gets you a discount. You have a fireplace, right?"

"Yup, sure do."

"Great, we'll bring a splitter and form some nice ranks of firewood for you too. We might all wind up working around each other and make a mess of your driveway, but at least that way your roofing crew can start. When Zak explained that part, we bumped you to the front of our line."

"I'm glad we bought all six chairs," Philip said, unable to be surprised Zak had gotten to know Henry, and by extension Henry knew him and then Tom, and that connection provided yet another solution to tackling this problem.

Henry laughed. "I promise we'll quote you a fair price. Friends and family, guaranteed."

"Charge what you're worth—Zak can handle it."

"Hah, I'll put that on the invoice. A couple of my crew are stoked we're headed to the little enchanted place in the woods, and for a football and tech star. Don't tell him, but I had no idea when we met."

"Me either, but he was onto me from the jump." Philip thought about his house being considered a little enchanted place in the woods, that anyone in the community considered it such, and smiled. "What time in the morning?"

"Early as we can make it, but no one has to be there to meet us. We'll get started and deal with the rest as we can." Henry said something muffled, and Philip picked up the sounds of chainsaws and grinding machinery. "And for now I gotta go."

"Great. I'm relieved to get someone I trust on it so quickly. Take care, man."

"Thanks, bud, you too. We'll get it put to rights."

Philip held his phone away as Henry answered someone in an indistinct yell and then the call ended.

He found his backpack, got some tote bags, and used the bed to sort things and pack for the foreseeable days. Small mercy that so much of Zak's stuff had migrated to his bedroom in the past weeks;

he packed all of it too. The urge to clean was hard to ignore, but he couldn't see what good it'd do and nothing irreplaceable would be lost.

Hearing birdsong and leaves in the breeze like he'd opened every window was a bit odd but also comforting. To them it was a normal day and the storm had passed.

Philip was carrying bags downstairs when Zak's truck crunched on the driveway. He smiled and ran outside and met Zak by the hood, and didn't stop until he was in Zak's arms. Zak gathered him in and crushed them close, and Philip shut his eyes.

"Long day?" Zak said facetiously.

"I've had worse." Philip shifted so he was tucked under Zak's arm and pressed a hand to Zak's chest. "Some good news is most of your stuff is fine, I didn't lose my laptop or externals, and everything downstairs is basically unscathed."

"And the bad news?"

"If the stair treads don't dry right, they'll definitely warp, the foyer decided to become a tidal basin, so that gets into subflooring, I'm worried that water infiltrated the center wall, and all my framed work is toast. But that one's a straightforward remedy—we're going to pick out new ones to hang."

"Are we? Okay." Zak tightened his arm.

They naturally started walking as they talked, to the felled tree because Philip needed to look at it again and Zak wanted to see, stooped under the trunk and surveyed the damage to the side of the house, and then continued on down the path.

"What made you go looking for slate roof guys?"

Zak reached into the lapel pocket of his raincoat and handed Philip his note from that morning.

The app idea is a good one. See you at home.

"When I woke up to you gone, I didn't assume anything dramatic, but that gave me just a little more to build on than just we'd meet up again." Zak made sure to get the note back and carefully tucked away again. "That and I started by searching for a roofer, any roofer. A storm of this magnitude meant I had to go pretty far afield, and then they were recommended. I figured why not with slate—it suits the house and they're available. And not looking to take advantage of someone who just lost their old roof."

"It's incredible the number and variety of predators who start circling immediately after disasters. There to price gouge or outright can't do the work. It's something I've seen a lot."

"Maybe there's a way to report on it from a personal angle. Say, by a well-respected journalist talking about it affecting his hometown."

"Great idea. If you know someone of that pedigree, send them my way."

"Speaking of, Tom already got and went over that newsletter contract. He said it's solid. Generous, even."

"Add that to the good news column, because I'm gonna need it." Philip anticipated spending too much of it on the house, the garden, but also that the words were there and the writing fulfilling again. "I'm also going to like the work."

"Good."

"Vultures, the excellent kind." Philip pointed them out, graceful sooty Vs wheeling in the distance. "That clean-up crew is going to be busy for a while too."

"To repeat, speaking of, contacted an old teammate—he played offense, ugh—who I remembered his dad being in construction. Turns out Curtis is now restoring historic mansions in Buffalo. He's coming down in a few days to draw up a quote and materials list, and then he and his crew will get started." Zak ran his hand along Philip's forearm and then held Philip's hand. "Let me pay for it. A gift, a thanks for letting me stay here, as a friend. Whatever makes sense to you."

Philip studied the interlaced fit of their fingers and then looked at the swollen river, the battered forest, the bright blue sky.

To his continued silence Zak added, "Let me pay for it but there's zero strings attached. If for no better reason than you know I care about this house and can easily afford it."

"I don't have much other choice, and sure no good ones, so I will." Philip pulled from Zak's hold and faced him. "But my acceptance does come with strings."

"Of course." Zak swallowed and nodded once, but then composed his expression to pleasantly neutral.

"Don't leave when the six months end. Six months after that, sign to own the house with me, not another contract. Take me to second breakfast whenever you want, but quit snaring me in town small talk and farmer's market social stuff. Always have passels of defense team kids here to do yard work I don't want to bother with. Let me exploit you for my newly inked and lucrative newsletter and likely book deal." Philip licked his lips and held Zak's gaze. "And love me at least half as much as I've come to love you."

Zak blushed very faintly but otherwise didn't react.

After what seemed an age, Philip said, "Well?"

"Well, most of what I've heard so far are total givens. I'm waiting for the conditions and demands."

Zak was so matter-of-fact it made him ask, "What weren't the total givens?"

"Putting me on the title."

"Hey, if you don't wan—"

Zak cut Philip off with a low, urgent noise and demanding kiss. Philip gave back, answered what Zak sought, and their kiss became exploratory, a revelation, and Zak laughed into it and then kissed him, hard, again and again.

Philip finally had to pull away and catch his breath, but Zak kept him close.

Brilliant sunset splintered the sky and the yard was smothered in gold.

Zak let Philip turn in his arms and he studied the house. "From this angle it doesn't look bad. Maybe we should just stay."

"No can do. I told Tom after we got what we needed we'd be back for a wellness check and dinner. Maria brought everything to make pasteles and tostones."

"Oh, yeah no. Definitely not, then."

Zak recaptured his hand and tugged him toward the house. Stopped midway up the path to kiss him and grope his butt and hold him tightly. Got moving but only to the patio, where he pulled Philip in to kiss until the sky had fallen dark.

Philip searched and found the moon. When he looked back at Zak he waited, because Zak had searched her out too. A mere sliver, a silvery cut against velvet, a high and distant new start.

"I love you too. Half as much and that much more," Zak whispered, and tilted their foreheads together.

They stood a while in reverie until Philip got them moving, grabbing their bags and then out front to Zak's truck.

He went to the passenger side and then stared at the house, the rounded door, the fieldstone, the collapsed walls and torn roof. "I would have lost all of this without you, you know."

"Well, I'd be lost without you." Zak smiled. "So I'd say that puts us at even."

"I need you—" Philip climbed into the cab and when Zak joined him, he finished, "to pay the last three months' rent now."

Zak lightly punched his arm, shook his head and cranked the truck, and burst out laughing when he turned onto the main road headed for the farm.

Three Months Later

"ALL RIGHT, Coach! We're ready!"

Philip rolled his eyes. "Once again, gentlemen, I am not a coach. I don't even like football."

"That must be why you're at all our home games." Braden grinned and looked across the yard at Zak. "Can we call you Mr. Coach, then?"

"No. No you may not." Philip shooed Braden away. "Go stand with the others so we can get this done."

The backyard teemed—the throngs he'd always wanted to avoid were here. The whole goddamn football team, Tom and Kelly and Madeline, some of the fire department, and the construction guys and their families, and Zak had warned him a few more random people might show up. Henry had arrived with a custom piece made from the smaller of the oak trees brought down in the storm, and helped Philip get it inside and placed just-so.

This would never be his favorite but he didn't mind. Was actually enjoying the day. Would be very glad when everyone was gone and it was only him and Zak and the cats again.

For at least a week. Possibly three.

Tom and the fire chief manned the grill. The boys were eating enough to feed a small country. Maddie got cooed over and passed around but mostly wanted to stick with Zak—or Philip. All this apparently in celebration of the football team's first win of the season, and in several years. Also because the house was completely fixed and Zak completely moved in, the newsletter had a healthy readership, and the app would soft launch soon.

Aside from the noise and disruption and more noise, the house had been generally livable during construction. Days without water or power Zak had taken him to Niagara Falls and then into the city, and even days with power they'd traveled to places Philip wanted to share and Zak wanted to see.

Curtis and his crew had done amazing work and Zak's blank check had allowed every extra amazing idea to happen. Weird attic spaces into another room, a pergola over the back patio and half of it a balcony for their bedroom, the foyer and stairs opened just enough to give entry to the kitchen. The house was as Philip had always envisioned—better— thanks to friends and friends-of and Zak a permanent fixture.

Thanks to letting the right people in, accepting and trusting their help, along with his own inner strength to work hard and see it through.

He posted about repairs on the house and what was happening in town to his socials and logged weekly stories for the newsletter. Both grew in readership and attention, and he'd been glad to recommend writers and reporters to expand the newsletter's roster, including getting Harriet on board. But he gave all credit to the explosive growth of his own account to Zak and their adoption of three cats, and documenting rehabbing the flooded animal shelter with the football team.

A glance at the house confirmed his expectation of finding Luna, Mitsuki, and Badr crowded on the bedroom windowsill to observe the proceedings, sleek and too smart littermate tabbies they both hopelessly adored.

Philip bobbled and braced forward on the top step. "Whoa, hey. Do you have the ladder or not?" He glared down at Tom.

"Yes, geez, I have the ladder. So take the pictures already—we're ready to cut the cake and we need the whole team to help carry it onto the patio."

"I would if you'd hang on so I don't faceplant." The football team had decided they wanted their official photo at the overlook. Philip thought on the field or something made more sense, but they were set on it.

Tom patted Philip's leg. "I'm right here."

Philip grumbled but then half smiled when Tom did. He gestured for everyone to crush closer together and framed the shot. Just as he hit the shutter, he found Zak and Zak winked.

"…you fucker," he muttered, checked the screen and shook his head, motioned at Zak to behave, and took the photo again.

He snapped several more to be certain and got a few good ones, gave the all clear, and then Tom helped him stow the ladder. Philip made a window check. The kitties were still there, so he got pictures of them too.

Tom followed his gaze. "I gotta say, it's pretty iconic of Zak, *the* most eligible bachelor in tech, to casually announce to the world he was shacked up with you—because he wanted to start posting about you guys' cats."

"That was… a moment."

"You gave him permission."

"Yes, because I'm with him but I don't own him."

"Maybe not in the empirical sense."

"Hmmph." Philip didn't argue that, though.

He had his share of being in the public eye over the years but only when a major story broke, and once that passed, he could slide right back into obscurity. Zak's photo of catching Philip in a surprise kiss while holding the then-tiny kittens in one hand and captioning it simply "my greatest loves" had stirred up controversy, speculation, and attention that lasted far longer than anything he'd ever endured. Zak had been as unruffled and confident as ever. Philip had been very glad to live way out of the way in a small, and tolerant, town.

"It's cool to be the close buddy of big-deal pollinator garden and animal shelter influencers." Tom slung an arm on Philip's shoulders. "The cachet I get from it means I never wait for a table at Barb's. And I think we've even become friends."

"Ooh, that is a big deal. Lucky you."

"My bestie moves to my hometown and lands an awesome boyfriend for me to finally have someone to appreciate football with? The luckiest."

Someone sent up a whoop and then cheering started as the football field cake with a tiny house sitting midfield made its grand entrance. Philip got some pictures but otherwise hung back in the shadow of the house as everyone else descended.

"It's almost the size of an actual field. How the hell did you and Zak get it here?"

"We hitched the small farm trailer to his truck." Tom held out his palms at Philip's disbelief. "No joke. One scrap lumber box made to fit the cake secured to the bed later, and we were off." He widened his eyes. "Slowly."

"Huh."

"Pretty sure the bakery made quarterly payroll from it alone."

"That and Zak keeping me in bear claws and lemon bars." Philip patted his middle. "It's a good thing I stay active."

Tom chortled.

"Man, whatever." Philip bit his lip but still smiled. "I meant the twice a week conditioning with the team you both talked me into and all the hikes Zak and I go on. Weirdo."

"And how!" Tom said without shame or apology. He made a rectangle with his thumbs and hands. "Listen, don't tell anyone but the cake is actually four cakes iced together. Four flavors too."

"That secret is safe with me." Philip watched Zak cut hunks loaded with icing from all four sides. "So wait, what flavors?"

"White, chocolate, lemon, and this mixed berry thing."

Philip eyed Zak's loaded plate in anticipation of it coming his way.

Tom snickered. "I knew you *like* liked him. Knew it all along."

"Yes, you're very smart and perceptive. Maybe rewarding yourself with some cake is in order."

"And just in time to be leaving as he gets over here."

"Oh, you leaving is worth three pieces of cake. At least."

Tom started walking and then half turned. "Don't forget, you've got Maddie on Friday so Kelly and I can have a date night. We plan on falling asleep during a movie."

"I couldn't possibly forget—you think that guy would let me?" Philip rolled his eyes and pointed at Zak on fast approach.

Zak lived for babysitting nights. Afternoons. Random mornings when Kelly needed an extra pair of hands around the house. Philip, well. He sure didn't hate them. Tom's folks would be in town soon to meet Maddie; Zak would probably wind up fighting them for baby duty.

He took the fork Zak offered and speared a bite of chocolate. Zak sidled right next to and then pressed to him, stood on the paver that jutted from the corner of the house, patio ahead of them, the dense and shady cut behind. Solar lights along the path and strands of them overhead came on as the last of the sun disappeared, dim and just right. Autumn had settled into the world, the forest across the river showing its first dusky blush as blooms faded in the garden. Philip reveled in the cool air, the crisp bite of the wind, the longer night cloaking them earlier and earlier.

Especially welcome after sweltering in the tropics, chasing the breaking crest of a story he and a reporter friend had scooped. He'd only gotten back yesterday.

"Doing okay?" Zak asked past a mouthful of berry cake.

Philip waved his fork around. "You could have done all this without me, that would have been fine."

"As if. One, the team never would have forgiven me. Two, who then exactly would take the team picture? And three, please."

They both knew he didn't mean it, same as they understood the necessary intricacies of his token protests and Zak's rebuttals. Philip pretended not to notice the warm span of Zak's hand pressing against his back after sneaking under his layers.

He had a big bite of lemon and considered doing something so obvious as making sure to get frosting on his cheek. "'S'good."

Zak hummed agreement but was more focused on the movements of his mouth and throat, when he licked his lips, as he sucked a crumb from his fingertip.

"I ordered lemon just for you."

"You're so nice to me."

Zak nodded, rubbed circles on his back, and landed a quick kiss to his temple. Philip smiled and lingered over another bite of lemon and then hollow-cheek worked at the icing stuck between the fork tines. Zak grunted, ditched the plate, and spun Philip around the corner to the side of the house. Philip's breath heaved when he hit the wall, the impact cushioned by Zak's arms, and then Zak pushed in and demanded a kiss, tilted his head to open his mouth wider, and kissed him again.

Philip gave, eagerly, and with his own busy hands and demands.

"Hey! Yo, Philip, where are ya—come get the fire going!" Tom called.

Philip had to grab hold of Zak's shoulders when Zak pulled, muttering a threat on Tom's well-being.

"Kinda your fault," he whispered, and kissed Zak with a promise of so much more once they were alone.

The fireplace was his thing. Set it, and then one match and lit, honed from years of camping and living rough in the field. Also, the fireplace was his—from Zak—so he didn't really like anyone else messing with it.

"My one regret," Zak intoned gravely and then laughed. He crunched free of the dying shade plants and tugged Philip until they were steady on the path, and then paused to lift and kiss Philip's hand. "I'm really glad you're back."

Philip smiled. "It's good to be home."

Keep reading for an excerpt from
Off-Map Hearts
by Elle Brownlee!

Chapter One

GRADEN SETTLED into one of the comfortable seats in the small lounge, checked his watch, and nodded with satisfaction. Twenty-five minutes until his chartered flight was scheduled to take him home to New York City. The perfect middle between not feeling rushed or waiting for hours.

He inventoried his carry-on and pockets—wallet, apartment keys, his favored lip balm so he didn't get too dried out—opened his planner, and fired up his laptop. He'd read once that waiting rooms were the perfect opportunity for digital tidying, and he'd followed that tip ever since.

There was a brief email from his manager that had nothing to do with the business he concluded yesterday. He shut down his laptop without sending a response.

Graden closed his eyes and opened them again. His gaze fell on his planner, open to next week when he'd expected this news—with a different outcome. An outcome he'd toiled for and deserved, along with more consideration than a terse email. He thought again how he was lucky to have a good job that used his talents, and swallowed his disappointment. Then he checked his watch again and frowned.

Ten minutes to takeoff and no one was at the desk or gate. He got up and looked out at the tarmac and alarm shot through him. There wasn't even a plane.

He reread his boarding pass and confirmed this was the correct gate, walked back up the hall and confirmed this was the correct terminal, and thumbed his phone and cross-checked with his planner to confirm he was here on the correct date.

A woman in uniform appeared farther down the hall and began readying a different gate.

"Excuse me?" Graden asked as he approached.

"Yes? Can I help you?" Her smile was practiced but reassuring. When she turned fully to him, her nametag caught the light.

"Hi, Angelica. Thank you, I hope so." Graden lifted both hands. "Thing is, I've never flown charter before, and I'm worried I've done something wrong."

"Welcome! I hope you enjoy it. You are in the private flights terminal, so that's a good start." She peered around. "And I know it seems quiet, but that's just in comparison to the commercial terminal. It's always like this. Who are you booked with?"

"Peregrine, today, to New York City."

Angelica's practiced smile faltered. "Oh." She shook her head. "I'm so sorry, but they're gone."

"Gone?"

An unintelligible shout interrupted whatever Angelica might have said in reply. Fast, heavy footfalls echoed in approach, and Graden turned to watch a large man juggling a disorganized assembly of stuff running toward the end of the terminal.

He seemed to take in the empty gate, and then Graden and Angelica, and skidded a U-turn to halt in front of them.

"Hi! Did the flight to NYC leave yet?" The guy fumbled a book, caught it, and then shoved a camera bag higher on the same shoulder that also supported a heavy tote. He seemed almost delighted at the prospect that the flight was already gone.

Maybe relieved. Definitely tall and broad in the shoulders and narrow in the hips, dinner-plate-spanning squared hands, greenish-hazel eyes bracketed by laugh lines lighter than his tan, and thick, sun-lightened and shaggy brown hair. He wore faded but sturdy cargo pants, hiking sandals, layers of T-shirts, and a very soft-looking flannel.

Not that Graden was cataloging anything. He was just a details person by nature.

"I have urgent business—" The guy pulled a face to suggest he didn't find it urgent. "—and got booked on it yesterday since it wasn't private."

Graden processed that. Even though he hadn't actively thought the charter was meant only for him, he hadn't considered he'd have company on the flight. He was oddly disappointed but intrigued.

"Are you waiting for it too?" the guy asked him.

"I was."

"Hah, for once I'm not the only late passenger."

"Unfortunately, neither of you are late. As I was explaining to this gentleman"—Angelica nodded to Graden—"I'm afraid it looks like your flight is never going to take off."

"Mechanical failure or something?"

"Or something. Apparently it's gone." Graden pulled his hands far apart. "All gone."

Angelica tutted. "Word is they've been having major financial problems but managed to book enough flights to last a bit longer." She raised her brows meaningfully. "When I got in this morning, the place was buzzing with gossip that everything's gone. I'm sorry no one thought to inform you. Bruce, your would-be pilot, didn't know either. He showed up and then left with the army of authorities who stripped Peregrine offices of every last stapler and even towed the plane away."

"Is there a different charter? Or…?" Graden asked.

"It doesn't work like getting bumped but getting a seat on a different plane. Sorry." She tapped her mouth with two fingers. "My flight is going to LA. Yours was the only one going east, but I have the contact information for the private carriers so you can inquire about booking with them. And if nothing else, I'll get a courtesy car to take you to the main terminal."

"That sounds like a good start. Thank you. Let me check on a few things first." Graden retrieved his belongings, stepped away to a tall table, and opened his planner to a blank sheet of paper.

He noticed his would-be travel companion remained chatting with Angelica, looking enviably unbothered.

Just in case, he started with Peregrine and wasn't surprised to get no answer. As it rang and rang, he wrote a quick punch list for who he'd need to contact and what he'd need to do to get home.

Next he called the company who had hired the consulting firm he worked with. The client had brought him to Las Vegas. They offered to reimburse him for the cost of a commercial flight, even first class. The charter was apparently a one-off because they'd had a friends-of discount but couldn't shed more light on the situation than that.

He searched available flights, including what swinging a different charter would cost. He let out a long, soundless gasp at the estimates— enough for a down payment on a house. So, definitely a commercial flight, then. He pushed aside the dread of securing a last-minute flight, neatly packed his things, and squared his shoulders.

"A car to the main terminal it is," he said when he got back to the desk.

"Hold up a minute," the guy said to Angelica and drew Graden aside. "Good news—my rental return is not processed yet, so we're still ready to roll."

"Okay," Graden said on elongated syllables. He wasn't sure why he needed to know this.

"It just hit me. You're here, I'm here, we both need to get to New York."

If that was an explanation, Graden was still completely in the dark.

He stuck out a hand. "Name's Cole, by the way."

"Graden," he said and took Cole's hand. It was as large and square in feel as appearance, strong and callused and warm, and the skin of their palms burred together when Cole pulled away. He suppressed a shiver. "Is the car here? Or at a return lot? You could simply take the courtesy car with me," Graden said, solving a problem Cole didn't seem worried by.

"No, it's here. The agency let me drop it direct since I was running late." Cole narrowed his eyes. "You look confused—annoyed? It's just over there." He poked a finger in the air to their left, indicating what, Graden didn't know.

"Why would taking the rental to the main terminal be better?" Graden's mind worked it over. "Are you going to get a hotel for the night or something? You don't have to go out of your way. I can get there on my own."

Cole's easy grin returned. "I don't mean drive to the terminal. I mean drive to New York."

"Drive to New York?" Graden repeated incredulously. "Just like that? Is that even possible?" The idea boggled. New York was more than half the country away.

"Yeah, why not? I love the open road, stopping to see cool stuff, encountering the unexpected. It's not even that far, really. I've done way longer. And—better than being cooped up in an airplane."

"Wait, you'd rather drive for days on end than spend a few hours on a plane?"

"Absolutely. It seemed rude not to offer since you're stuck same as me. So, what do you think?"

"That I don't even know you." Graden said the first thing that came to mind. "You don't know me."

The next thing that came to mind was a small, rebellious voice saying he wouldn't mind getting to know Cole, but he didn't add that part.

"You're organized. You get to the airport early. You still travel dressed up." Cole lifted his chin to indicate Graden's dress pants and button-down shirt. "That and my gut tells me it'll be okay, and I listen to my gut."

"I'm more of a facts and figures guy, myself." Graden remembered a detail from before. "Isn't your business in New York urgent?" He shook his head. "It seems as if a long drive wouldn't be the best solution here."

"A fair point. One sure to be made when I finally arrive." Cole laughed but without humor. "Yeah, sorry. I'm sure you just want to get— home?"

Graden nodded.

"Right, right. I probably shouldn't have even offered, but…." He shrugged again, and his gaze dropped from Graden's eyes to his mouth and quickly back up again.

So quickly Graden almost didn't believe it happened.

"Anyway, here's to this morning using up your quota of daily troubles, and you have smooth sailing from here. Take care, okay? Angelica," Cole said louder. "Thanks for your help." He gathered his stuff and started walking away before Graden could answer.

"You too," he called and winced. He rolled his eyes at his lack of imagination or ability to ask for more on Cole's plans for driving cross-country or stall to get a bit more time together. Which was ridiculous to even consider. A stranger met at an airport while under stress? Not exactly ideal.

His phone buzzed before he could think of something memorable to add in parting.

Messages appeared, so many and so rapidly he only got the gist as they piled up. All from his manager. Asking him to take on extra work— to do and fix the job of someone else—and wanting his Vegas wrap-up.

Graden unlocked his phone, and curiosity made him open a browser and search *drive from Las Vegas to New York City*. His eyes widened at the distance. The route went through so many of the huge, square states he'd never been in or given much thought to before. But once he got over the shock, he saw it wouldn't even take two full days. Well, it probably would take two full days as they'd have to make stops, but it wasn't quite as colossal a trek as he'd imagined. He navigated the route and was heartened to see it was major interstates with several big cities along the way.

Dinner in Denver with Cole would be nice.

He huffed, but something pulled his attention to the corridor. Cole wasn't quite out of sight yet, but he shook his head. What was he even thinking?

There were two flights he should move on, an almost-full red-eye and an almost-full first thing tomorrow morning. The idea of a middle seat and early-morning arrival or having a restless night before a middle seat and commuter-hour arrival killed his soul a little, but there wasn't much to be done about that.

The red-eye seemed the lesser evil—just get it over with—and he wanted to be sure of the details to know where the courtesy car should take him. As he tapped a drop-down menu, his phone changed windows, because instead he'd tapped a message notification that had simultaneously appeared.

More messages arrived, from his manager and the coworker his manager prompted him to "advise," expectantly taking him for granted.

Graden wasn't quick with a temper or frustration, but when the slow burn of either began, it ran hot and deep.

He turned off notifications. He reread the brief email from his boss, stifled hurt and guilt and the pull to blame himself, and turned his out-of-office message back on. He closed every tab with possible flight information and the terminal map.

"Angelica? I won't be needing a courtesy ride, thank you. And thanks for answering my questions and giving me something to go on. I hope you have a good flight to LA."

"Good luck with the rest of your travels." Angelica waved as she bustled about.

Graden made sure he had everything. A couple days in a car with some time to think and more importantly get over himself didn't seem like a bad idea.

The completely different appeal of spending a few days in a car with Cole was something that he probably shouldn't think about too much.

"Hey," he said more to himself, and then he shoved his phone into his pocket and chased after Cole.

Cole had disappeared. Graden hurried until he burst outside. He looked left, that vague direction Cole had indicated before, and his heart thumped faster when he caught sight of the tall, disheveled figure, almost to the end of the sidewalk aproning the terminal and about to go inside.

"Cole?" he shouted and kept speed walking, glad there were so few people around.

He made to call again, but Cole cocked his head and slowed, and then turned.

Graden's breath returned to him.

"Yes, I'll go," Graden said across the distance, as if Cole would disappear if he didn't get the words out. "With you, I mean."

Cole's eyes narrowed and he made a quick scan of Graden's person, briefly closed his eyes, and then stood there biting the corner of his lip.

Graden got two steps away and stopped. "That's if the offer is still open, of course. I'm sorry if I bothered you," he added by habit.

"What?" Cole seemed to shake loose of something. "Oh—yeah, of course, of course it is. Don't be sorry. What changed your mind?"

Graden couldn't tell if Cole was pleased or grumpy that he'd decided to tag along, and his spurt of brave purpose deserted him.

"No good flights," he said flatly. He sighed without realizing as a litany of things ran through his mind. Anger at his boss. Bitter disappointment. The brand-new inkling that life wasn't as square-cornered perfect and going to plan as he'd thought. "Lots of reasons."

Something made Cole smile, softer than his wide grin, and nod in understanding.

SCAN THE QR CODE
BELOW TO ORDER!

Elle Brownlee always followed her creative, adventuring spirit. Growing up she loved reading, watching Westerns, and taking long hikes, where she'd craft miniature worlds with moss and rocks while making up stories of what happened there. As an adult, not a lot has changed. She still loves all these things—which makes being a writer such a joy. She also loves rainy days in autumn, National Parks, birding and quilting and stickers, and the perfect cup of tea.

Elle currently juggles plenty of travel, working to make the world a better place, and writing. She's so thankful to be able to share her work with a growing audience, and especially grateful to have you reading along.

Website: www.ellebrownlee.com/index.html
Facebook: www.facebook.com/elle.brownlee
Twitter: @ellebrownlee
Email: brownlee.elle@gmail.com

Follow me on BookBub

SAY YES TO A MESS

Elle Brownlee

Can a fake engagement become *Yes, I Do?*

Can a fake engagement become a real marriage?

Wiley Grey is stuck in a rut. He loves his picturesque hometown, helping in his best friend's bakery, and the house his grandmother left him. But something's missing.

Holt Leydon never intended to become a reality TV show host. When his flamboyant brother, Kit, needed a handyman on the set of I Do!, Holt fell into the role, using his expertise to make Kit's wildest wedding designs come true. Now he's ready to move on. Kit has agreed on one condition: they rescue Kit's would-be ratings bonanza "coming home" episode by making Holt the groom.

The problem is Holt needs someone to marry, and fast. Something compels him to ask childhood friend Wiley—and Wiley agrees to the pretense.

Kit gets his dramatic last episode, Holt gets off the show, and Wiley gets some artificial excitement and a "honeymoon" on the show's dime. It's perfect—until the grooms start wishing their pretend engagement was more reality and less TV....

Scan the QR Code
Below to Order!

DREAMSPUN DESIRES
A COAST GUARD RESCUE NOVEL
STAGGERED COVE STATION
Elle Brownlee
Rescues are wild in the Alaskan terrain.
So is romance.

A Coast Guard Rescue Novel

Rescues are wild in the Alaskan terrain. So is romance.

Sun-kissed California guardsman Dan Farnsworth might be at home in the water, but he's out of his element at remote, rugged, and freezing Staggered Cove Station. Acclimating proves hard enough, but he's also digging into how the station's previous rescue swimmer was lost at sea. Was it an operation gone bad or something more sinister? Add to that the instant tension between him and his partner—no-nonsense Alaska-born Karl Radin—and Dan has his hands full.

As his investigation heats up, so does the attraction between Dan and Karl, even if they don't completely trust each other. But as suspicious events escalate to sabotage, Dan starts to fear that he and Karl won't get the chance to become more than reluctant coworkers.

SCAN THE QR CODE
BELOW TO ORDER!

TWO FOR TRUST

Elle Brownlee

A fairy-tale vacation—if he can get the ending right.

A fairy-tale vacation—if he can get the ending right.

American nurse Finch Mason steps beyond the comfort of his orderly life and takes a dream trip to England, complete with a National Trust Pass so he can visit numerous historical sites. At the first one on his list, he's warmly welcomed—and told he bought a pass good for two.

Finch doesn't hesitate to offer the pass to Benedict, a handsome Brit also there on an outing. They spend a magical week touring the countryside, and while it's too soon to get attached, Finch wishes their time together would never end.

Then Finch finds himself stuck abroad with no money, and he has no one to turn to but Benedict. Benedict is happy to help, but he also owes Finch some answers—such as who he really is and why he was at the estate where they first met.

SCAN THE QR CODE
BELOW TO ORDER!

Drawn
ELLE BROWNLEE

Sebastian (Sen) Holt is an artist currently in New Orleans. He's always been a wanderer, believing in fate and following signs to guide his destiny. Although he itches to pull up stakes, getting a painting into a gallery keeps him rooted. One morning his good friend calls him in desperate need of help with her cleaning business. Her regular cleaner flaked, she can't lose her client, and there's no one else.

The job is at a large and recently restored house—and the owner, Morgan Ballard, comes home unexpectedly. They are immediately drawn together, as if they know each other, but they've never met. As they grow closer, Morgan behaves like two people. Sometimes he's friendly and casual, and other times intimate and demanding. Sen juggles his painting through bursts of vision-like inspiration, the cleaning job, and an unexpected commission—all while trying to unlock the growing mystery of the intense connection he feels to Morgan. He's not sure which scares him more—the strangeness surrounding their growing bond or that he's found someone to make him reconsider his lifelong wanderlust.

SCAN THE QR CODE
BELOW TO ORDER!

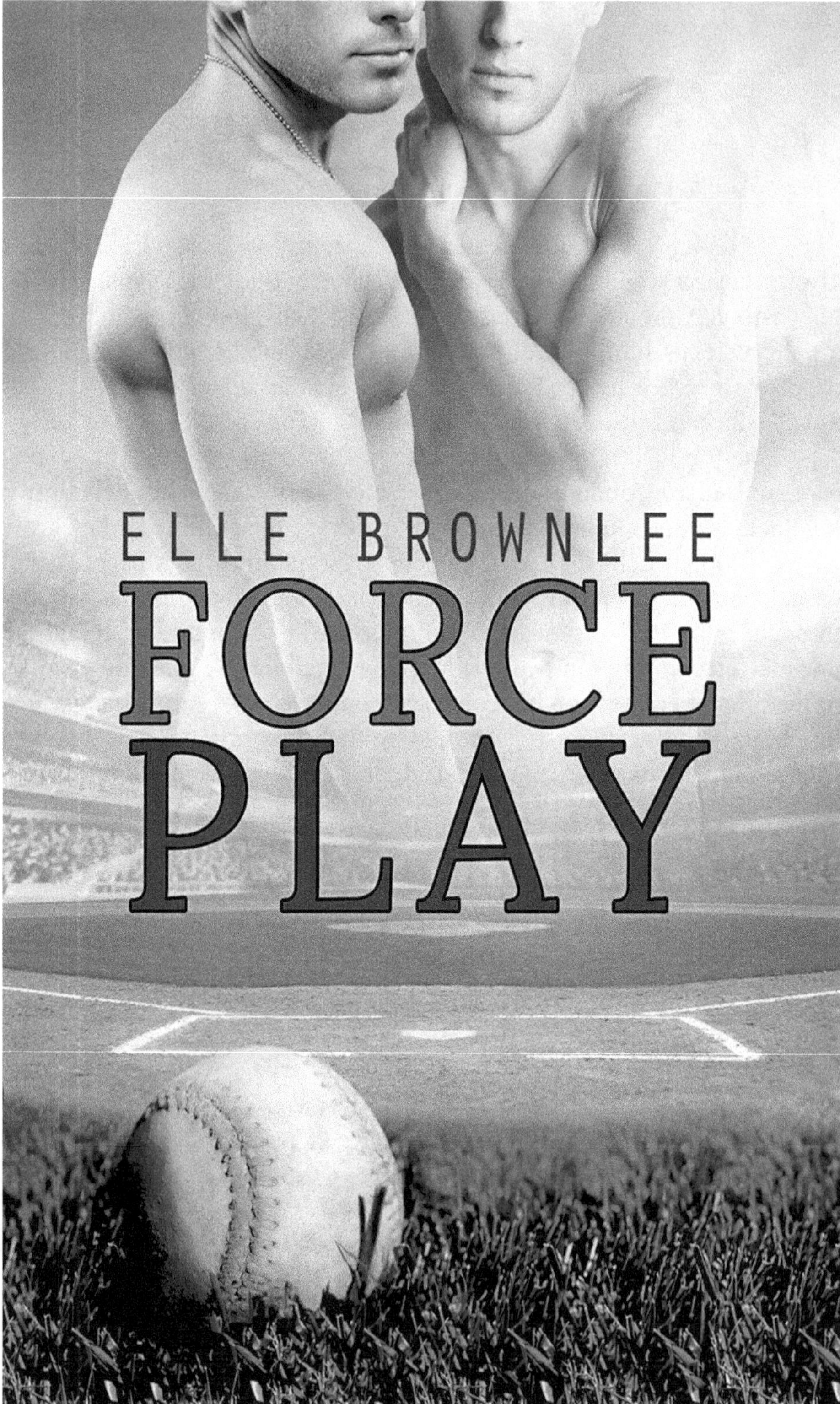
ELLE BROWNLEE
FORCE PLAY

Professional baseball player Harmon "Hawk" Kiel was a rookie sensation with dazzling talent and an arrogant attitude to match. But he's hit his sophomore slump, and his natural talent seems to have deserted him, along with the confidence of his team and the media's approval. During the All-Star Break, he hits rock bottom, gets careless, and sensational pictures of him at gay clubs go viral. All at once he's outed—and out of a job.

When he's dealt to the Loggerheads, a worse-than-terrible expansion team in Charleston, South Carolina, he can't imagine he'll get a warm reception—nor does he particularly want one. But it's the only chance at redemption he has.

There he meets Caleb Jackson, a former player who's part of the Loggerheads organization, someone who tries to be the friend Harmon so desperately needs. But Caleb has a secret too, one more gut-wrenching than anything Harmon can imagine. Together they try to put the past behind them, rediscover their love of the game, and maybe even find the love of their lives.

SCAN THE QR CODE
BELOW TO ORDER!

FOR **MORE** OF THE **BEST** **GAY** ROMANCE

www.ingramcontent.com/pod-product-compliance
Lightning Source LLC
Chambersburg PA
CBHW071528120726
47907CB00013B/1263